HIS *Savage* WAS HER *Weakness* 2

A NOVEL BY

TYA MARIE

PROLOGUE

Shahani

I touched down in New York City with a heavy heart. The week I spent with Sampson consisted of making love, exploring the city, and being treated like a queen. I had amassed a whole new wardrobe, with every item of clothing picked out by Sampson, who had an amazing eye for detail. Since I couldn't take them to my place, Sampson carried them to his place where according to him, they had a special spot of their own. *I can't believe he's given me a spot in his closet,* I thought with a laugh as I stared out the window, watching Brooklynites head to work on this bleary Friday morning. My thoughts were interrupted by my Uber skidding to a stop, slamming me into the passenger seat.

"What the fu—what happened up there?" I asked once I saw the ambulance and police cars filling the block.

The driver shook his head. "I have no idea. I'll have to back up and—"

"Wait," I said, catching sight of the purse on the ground. "Pull up a little more."

"The cops are going to stop me—"

"Just pull up some more. I think I know the person that bag belongs to," I said, giving the passenger seat an impatient slap.

The driver did as I requested, pulling up as close as he could before a uniformed cop stopped him. I jumped out of the car and darted past the cop, his shouts for me to stop falling on deaf ears. Another cop caught me before I could pick up the purse, commanding me to get behind the yellow tape because it was a crime scene. I shrugged out of his grip and turned in time to see Nubia being placed into an ambulance.

"Nubia!" I screamed, running to the ambulance. I was only a few feet away before a few more cops showed up and grabbed me, asking me what relation I was to Nubia. "I don't have time for these questions, just tell me where the fuck you're taking her!"

"Ma'am, we need to know—"

"I don't give a fuck what you need to know," I wailed over the sound of the ambulance sirens as it pulled off. "What hospital are they taking her to?"

A sergeant came over to me with his hands out as if to calm me down, "Ma'am, your friend was beaten within an inch of her life, and the person that did this is still at large. The more information we get right now, the better chances we have of catching whoever did this. Did your friend have any enemies?"

"Nubia is a good person. She wouldn't hurt a fly," I said, slapping my hand over my mouth to keep from crying like a baby. "I don't know who would do something like this. Can you please tell me where they're taking her?"

The sergeant knew he wasn't going to get much out of me while I was an emotional wreck. He told me that due to her injuries, Nubia would be taken to the nearest trauma hospital. I took off without a backwards glance, hopping back into my Uber and firing off the address to Woodhull Hospital. So many questions swirled through my mind, the main one being, *what happened?* I called Donovan and gave him the rundown. He promised to meet me at the hospital along with Nia, who might have some information on who could've done this. Nubia didn't have any other family for me to call, save for one person, and since I had a gut feeling he was behind this, I didn't want to give him any knowledge I was coming for that ass.

"Excuse me," I said once I reached the information desk at the hospital. "My friend was just admitted into the emergency room. Her name is Nubia Morris. Who can I talk to for an update on her information?"

Armed with information and instructions to sit in the waiting area until someone came to speak to me, I took refuge in a corner. All I could think of was how I left my friend alone for a week, knowing she had been through some serious shit in the name of a nut. Vincent saw an opening and took it, nearly snatching Nubia's life because I was slacking. I was replaying the thought of seeing her being loaded into the back of that ambulance when I spotted Donovan and Nia walking towards me. I was on my feet in an instant, rushing over to them and giving them a piece of my mind.

"I left her alone with the two of you, and you let Vincent attack her?" I hissed, looking around to make sure no one was listening. "Nia, you saw how she looked when we found her in Florida. What would make you think it was okay to let her go walking around alone that early in the morning?"

"Because she had been for this entire week, and ain't shit happen to her," Nia shot back. "If you felt so strongly about us watching her, then you should've taken her to Chicago with you. I killed a whole bunch of my own fucking kids so I wouldn't have to look after them."

Donovan helped me into a seat and said calmly, "Shorty been good this entire week. You already know plenty of niggas on the block fuck with me. I got them asking around to see if anyone saw someone that looked out of placed this morning. If it's her husband, then we'll handle him."

"I wouldn't be the least bit surprised if it was. She was out with some guy she bumped into at the club, and it definitely didn't go unnoticed," Nia said with a knowing look. "I'm willing to bet Vincent saw those pictures all over IG and pulled up on her."

My neck snapped to Nia. "You let her go off with a man she barely knows? Where were you?"

The usually smart-mouthed Nia, replied, "I was with a friend. Besides, she didn't hesitate to leave with him so they must be acquainted to a certain point."

I wanted to tell Nia how ridiculous she sounded, but I knew it wasn't true. The only reason I was snapping on her was because I had fucked up. Nubia thought of me as her protector, and I ditched her for some dick. I should've taken her with me to Chicago, and now I knew

4

better. The next time I had business to handle she'd be right behind me, whether she liked it or not. Donovan comforted me as we waited in a strained silence, and I had started to breathe easy again when a doctor came out and called, "Family of Nubia Morris?"

"Right here," I said, nearly tripping over my feet to get to the doctor. "Please tell me she pulled through."

"Mrs. Morris is fine. We ran a few tests and discovered no signs of internal bleeding. However, she did suffer from a minor concussion, along with some superficial bumps and bruises. We'll be keeping her overnight for observation."

"Can we see her?"

"Being that she's with the police right now, I can only allow one of you up at this time," the doctor replied apologetically.

Donovan pecked me on the cheek. "How about you go upstairs, spend some time with her, and I'll pick you up later? We'll be back to visit with her later on."

I paced the entire elevator ride up, bracing myself for how she would look. I've seen Nubia after being mentally fucked up by Vincent, where she'd lost so much weight her clothes hung off of her, but this was a whole new level of damage being done. I came up on her room quietly, listening to the conversation she was having with the two detectives. They were pressing hard for any information on her attacker, and like a true victim of domestic violence, Nubia wasn't giving them anything. Normally I would be mad at her for protecting Vincent's bitch ass, but this time I would use it to my advantage.

"She said she doesn't know anything," I said, interrupting the borderline interrogation.

The detectives, a man and a woman, snapped their heads to me. The woman, a bottle blond with kind blue eyes said, "Any small detail that your friend knows, even the color of the car her attacker drove off in, would help us find him."

"You didn't get any of that from witnesses?" I countered, knowing someone had to have seen something if the police were called.

The male detective shook his head. "There were no witnesses. Right now we're working solely off of the word of Nubia."

"And like I said for the thousandth time: I didn't see who attacked me. I was walking to the grocery store when someone got me from behind," Nubia said, and I felt my legs give out from under me at the sight of her.

Nubia's left eye was swollen shut and her right had a blood clot in it. Her lip had been busted open, revealing where the blood on the ground came from. Dark bruises covered her arms, along with welts, and I could see tiny little cuts that came from a diamond ring. How did I know? Because those were the same marks that Donovan's girls had whenever he disciplined them while wearing his diamond pinky ring. This had Vincent all over it, and I prayed that Nubia wouldn't lie to my face when I asked her who did this once the cops were gone.

"Nubia wouldn't lie about something this serious," I said, holding on to the empty hospital bed behind me and taking a seat on the edge of it. "If she said she didn't see who attacked her, then she didn't."

The detectives glanced at Nubia, who nodded and replied, "You don't think I would want whoever did this put in jail? They're out there on the streets, and I feel like a sitting duck."

"Well, if anything comes to mind, Mrs. Morris, please let us know," the female detective said, inclining her head at me and following her partner from the room.

Once they were gone we sat there staring at each other, with me waiting for Nubia to say something, anything that would make this make sense. After five minutes of this staring contest, I relented, asking her for the real story. Part of me, the small part that knew Nubia had been under Vincent's wing long enough to be brainwashed by him, expected her to lie to me to protect him. However, Nubia opened up and told me the truth.

"I was on my way to the supermarket to grab some stuff for breakfast when Vincent rolled up on me cussing and screaming how he saw pictures of me with Maine on the Internet. I talked back to him, and next thing I knew, he was out the car beating the living daylights out of me. I tried running away, but he was too quick. He got me on the ground and was beating me like he wanted to…like he wanted to kill me. I was sure he did until I woke up in here."

"You don't have to worry about his bitch ass," I said, lowering my voice. "Because when I get my hands on him, I'm going to put a bullet in his head."

"Shahani, leave him alone," Nubia warned, and I could see she was genuinely frightened of Vincent possibly hurting me. "Please just leave him be. I'll handle this myself."

I didn't want to stress her anymore, so I said, "Fine, I'll leave him alone."

"Shahani, I know when you're lying to me. Leave him alone."

I rose from my seat with my hands in the air. "I promise not to lay a hand on Vincent. Now that we've got that out the way: would you like something to eat?"

I could tell Nubia thought I was bullshitting, but her hunger won out. "Yeah, are you going down to the cafeteria?"

"Girl, I'm running to that restaurant across the street to grab some real breakfast," I said, hiking my purse up on my shoulders. "What would you like?"

Nubia gave me her order, and I was off to handle my business. I called Donovan, who had only made it down the block, so he could double back and pick me up. Ten minutes later, we were speeding towards Vincent and Nubia's DUMBO apartment building. I didn't have Mercy, but Donovan always kept a burner on him just in case something popped off with his girls who did early morning servicing. I had him drop me off down the block just in case shit popped off and I had to make a quick getaway. The way these security cameras were set up, they'd have a BOLO on us in minutes.

"Good afternoon," the doorman said as he let me into the building. "Who am I buzzing you up to see?"

"I'm here to see Vincent Morris. His wife is in the hospital, and we haven't heard from him," I said, pretending I was in distress. My pretend nervousness and real tear-stained cheeks sold the look. "I know I'm probably not on the list, but this is an emergency. Can you bend the rules just this once?"

The doorman, who must've had a pretty good idea of how Nubia was treated, looked sympathetic as he pressed the elevator to let me upstairs. I rolled my shoulders on the ride up, stretching because there was no room for pulled muscles when you had business to handle. I knocked on Nubia's house door real polite, like a deliveryman or something, and delivered a blow to the face to the bitch that answered the door. She hit the floor with a thud, flailing around as she tried to make sense of what happened.

"Please," she cried, holding her face as she sat up. "Take whatever you want, just please don't hurt me."

I closed the door behind me and locked all three locks. "Bitch, I don't want any of your shit. I want your boyfriend, Vincent."

Shorty looked up and went from a frightened victim to incredulous. "I know you ain't show up here on some tough shit like Vincent doesn't already owe you an ass whupping."

"He owes me an ass whupping?"

"When he gets here he's going to bury you in the ground, bitch."

I admired my freshly done coffin nails, the matte burgundy looking flawless under this bright lighting. Was this bitch really worth me ruining my full set from Chicago? She wasn't, which was why I stomped her ass in the chest, knocking her back. I was on her before she could make another move and had my hand on her mouth in case she wanted to be bold and start screaming. I whipped out my gun and pressed it underneath her chin, immobilizing her instantly.

"I am going to move my hand from your mouth, and if you make one peep, I'll blow your fucking brains out. Am I making myself clear, or do I have to use another form of persuasion?"

I moved my hands, waiting for her to answer me. "What the fuck do you want?"

"I want Vincent. He beat the shit out of Nubia and damn near killed her. She's sitting in a hospital bed looking like she got hit by a car, and I know your 'boyfriend' has something to do with it."

She shrugged. "I haven't seen Vincent since early this morning. He said he had to handle some business at the shop, and I'm pretty sure that's where he is."

"Okay," I said, drawing out the word. "We'll go with that for right now. That he's at the shop handling business at the same time his wife was being beaten to death. I need you to give him a message for me when he returns."

"What is that?"

I grabbed my gun by the barrel, raised the butt and proceeded to pistol whip that bitch, knocking her in both of her eyes and giving her one good blow to the cheek, causing a fake tooth to pop out. She started crying out for help and little did she know, that's where she fucked up. I stood up and kicked her in the stomach, taking her breath away the same way Nubia's was taken by Vincent. She instinctively curled into a ball, giving me more leeway to handle her ass. A groan escaped her lips as I gave her a swift kick in the back.

"Please," she wheezed, attempting to crawl away from me. "Please, leave me alone."

I placed my foot on her back, pressing her into the floor and leaving her unable to move. "Tell Vincent that if he ever thinks to lay a hand on Nubia ever again, I will come back and slice and dice you. Do you understand me?"

"Yes," she cried, laying her head on the floor in defeat.

A bigger person would've left her suffering ass where she was, deciding that the message was received. However, an image of Nubia bruised and abused flashed into my mind, reminding me that this bitch had no problem reaping the rewards of my friend's misery. I lifted my gun again and knocked the bitch unconscious. Knowing a hothead like Vincent, he would be gunning for me soon, and he better come strapped because I was liable to put a bullet in his head on sight.

Nubia

Everything hurt. My legs were sore, every blink took extra strength I didn't have, and my body as a whole felt terrible. Yet nothing hurt more than knowing Vincent could hate me so much that he would try to kill me. Or at least I thought that's what he was trying to do. I would have to ask him whenever he chose to reach out to me. Yes, I was positive that Vincent would contact me, not out of love, but because he would want to know whether or not I told the police he was responsible for putting me in the hospital. With every passing day, I grew farther and farther from the once invested detectives taking my case seriously. They stopped calling, and I knew it was only a matter of time before the case was closed, and they moved on to someone who really needed their resources. I thought Shahani would be livid at me for hiding the truth, but she had been cool so far, not even mentioning Vincent.

"You're a grown ass woman, and I can't tell you how to live your life," she said on the following morning I was released. "But I can tell you that if you even think about getting back with Vincent, he will kill you."

I knew that was a fact, and other than my hideous face, it was the reason why I had been hiding in the house for a week. There was no cooking or cleaning for me—Shahani wouldn't allow it—giving me time to think of my next steps. I was still mulling over my course of action when Shahani said the unthinkable.

"Nubia, the door."

I sat up abruptly, sending a sharp pain jolting through my body, and plopped back down. "Who is it?"

"Maine," she mouthed, then whispered, "What do you want me to tell him?"

"I'm not here," I whispered back.

Shahani opened the door and spoke to Maine in her bougie ass manager's voice. "Nubia isn't in at the moment. Would you like for me to take a message?"

"Tell her I dropped by and give her this—my number is on the back," I heard Maine say.

Shahani waved the card in her hand. "I'll be sure to pass this along to her. Have a great night." She had barely turned the locks in place when she asked, "Why are you hiding from him? He seems to be the only decent nigga you've met in recent history."

"Look at my face, Shahani. He was ready to kill Vincent when we saw each other in Miami. If he saw this, Vincent would be good as dead."

"I don't see why that's a problem," Shahani said with a shrug. "Why…you're not seriously thinking about going back to him, are you?"

"No, I'm not. I just…I need to talk to him."

"Nubia, the last time you had words with that bitch ass nigga you almost ended up sharing words with Jesus. You don't need to say a damn thing to him."

I motioned to her couch. "And live on your couch for the rest of my life? Shahani, I might not want anything to do with him, but he can set me up with enough to get a small place."

"I can set you up with your job back at KFC. Vincent treats you the way he does, because at the end of the day, he knows you need him. Stop depending on him for stability that you can provide yourself."

"I have every right to depend on him because he's my husband. That's how marriage works," I said with more venom than I intended.

Shahani bit her lower lip like when she was itching to say something. "Fine, *Mrs. Morris.* Do what you want."

"Shahani—"

Shahani was on her feet and halfway across the living room before I could finish my sentence. She slammed her bedroom door shut, making the entire conversation that much more awkward. I felt bad for partially throwing my marriage up in Shahani's face, but there was no other way to explain this situation to her. As of right now, I did need Vincent more than I wanted to admit. He was no good to me dead, and as of right now, I was praying he stayed alive more than he was.

******

Shahani's sour mood continued over the next few days, with her barely exchanging more than a "Good morning" and "Good night" on her way to and from work. Her silent treatment was eating me up inside, and I couldn't take it anymore. The soreness from the attack had eased, and I was going to get back to pulling my weight like I promised.

Nia must've missed my cooking because when I asked her if she could pick some stuff up while she was out shopping, she didn't hesitate to put her hand out for the shopping list. I cleaned the house from top to bottom as a maple glazed chicken baked and pot roast simmered. Once I was done cleaning, I hooked myself up with a long shower and deviated from the tee and sweatpants combo I had been sporting since the hospital. If she was surprised when she got home, Shahani didn't say anything, simply noting that it was good to see me up and about on her way to her room.

"It's not you," Nia said as she helped me bring the food to the table. "Over the past few days she's been in her feelings over something. What, I have no idea, but don't let her sour ass mood get to you."

Shahani finally emerged from her bedroom wearing sweats and an oversized tee. She joined us at the table, making small talk until I decided to pipe up and apologize. The one thing I loved about Shahani was that she was able to forget as easily as she forgave.

"I know you didn't mean it the way it sounded," she said as she helped herself to the feast in front of us. "I'm going through my own shit, and it bled over a little into our relationship. I'm sorry about that."

"Don't be," I said, waving away her apology as I filled my plate with food. "I've also been thinking of your offer to get me my job back at KFC, and if you still can, I'll definitely be there once the rest of my face is done clearing up."

Shahani gave me one of her most genuine smiles I've seen in the past few days. "Of course, boo. You know I always got your back."

The mood at the table lightened, and we were in the middle of making plans for the following weekend when there was a knock at the door. Shahani motioned for Nia to answer the door while she went over to her purse and placed her hand inside of it. Nia mouthed "cops," sobering Shahani instantly. She closed her purse and went back to sitting at the table as Nia opened the door.

"Good evening, we're looking for Nubia Morris," I heard one of the officers say. "She wrote this down as the address where she could be reached."

Nia opened the door wider, allowing two detectives to step into the apartment. Their eyes traveled around the place studying the couch where my blanket and pillows were neatly arranged with my duffle bag at the side of the couch, to the spread of food, and finally resting on me. Most of the swelling had gone down, and the bruises could easily be covered with makeup whenever I was ready to leave the house again. I didn't know whether the look they gave each other was good or bad, but I guess I would soon find out.

"Good evening, Mrs. Morris," the older detective said with a friendly smile, attempting to build a bond with me because we were black. "I'm Detective Harper and this is my partner, Detective Scully. We'd like to talk to you about your husband, Vincent Morris. When was the last time you spoke to him?"

"I haven't seen Vincent since I left him in Miami," I said, motioning to Shahani. "I've been staying at my friend's house ever since. I haven't even gone home to grab clothes."

Detective Harper took a seat next to me, his dark eyes kind and sympathetic. "Mrs. Morris, as of right now, your husband is missing,

16

and we'd like to know if there's anyone you can think of that might know his whereabouts."

"How do you know he's missing?" Shahani asked.

Scully spoke up, his alert blue eyes studying Shahani for her reaction. "We know he's missing because his shop in Harlem was shot up, with ten people injured and five pronounced dead. In the midst of it all, five people watched as Mr. Morris was dragged from his shop with a shoulder wound."

"What?" I said, covering my mouth in horror.

"Yes, your husband is injured, and time is of the essence if we're going to find him before his situation grows grave. I know you mentioned that you haven't spoken to him in quite a while, but from the last conversation you had, is there anyone that would want to see him hurt?"

I shrugged. "Vincent kept me in the house and out of his business. I don't know who would do something like this."

"Weren't you attacked recently?" Scully asked, taking a measured look at my face.

"Yes, I was."

Scully ran a hand though his hair, his fingers nearly disappearing in the brunette locks. "Funny. You were attacked and then your husband's shop was shot up. Someone is really mad at the two of you."

"Nubia answered your questions, so now it's time for you to leave," Shahani said, pointing to the door. Harper tried to speak up, dismissing his partner's claim, which Shahani shut down completely.

"When you have questions or a suspect, please feel free to come back and ask as many questions as you want, but for right now, you need to leave my home."

Shahani closed the door and leaned against it, taking a few deep breaths then returning to her seat. I nearly lost my appetite at the news of Vincent's disappearance. What could have happened to him? Was he still alive? Would the police keep looking at me as the culprit when I've been nothing but the victim? These questions ran through my mind through dinner and after I called it a night and was tucked into bed. The questions eased me into a fitful sleep, which was interrupted by Shahani shaking me awake.

"What's going on?" I asked, staring around the dark living room in confusion. "Is everything okay?"

"Be dressed in five minutes," she whispered.

I dressed quickly, less out of excitement and more because I wanted to know what was going on. Shahani hadn't spoken more than six words to me over the past few days, and one visit from the cops has her dragging me out the house in the middle of the night on a mission? She didn't even look the least bit surprised at the news of Vincent's disappearance. I barraged her with these questions once we were in the privacy of her car. She studiously ignored me the entire ride, singing along with the radio or bopping her head to the beat.

"Listen," she said as we grew close to a part of Brooklyn I was unfamiliar with. "I may have overstepped my boundaries and made some moves on your behalf, but I didn't think it would be this serious."

"Shahani, what are you trying to tell me?"

We pulled up to a deserted warehouse that could easily come from an episode of *Power*. There were a couple of cars parked out front, one being a white van. My stomach sunk at the sight because I already knew what Shahani planned to tell me; I just needed to hear the words from her mouth.

"Nubia—"

"Shahani, did you have something to do with Vincent going missing?"

"I...well..."

"Is he dead?" I said, my throat growing tight. "Shahani, please don't tell me you brought me here to see his body..."

"You know what? I can show you better than I can tell you," Shahani replied, climbing out of the car.

I knew she couldn't stand Vincent from the moment I introduced them to each other, but I couldn't believe that Shahani would mess around and have him killed. I was ready to write off her and our entire friendship until I saw Vincent bound and gagged, kneeling on a tarp spanning a good portion of the empty warehouse. He begged me with his eyes to free him, and I almost made a move to when Maine appeared out of thin air, a machete in his hand.

"Maine, what the fuck!" I shouted, storming over to him and grabbing his wrist as if to take his machete away from him. "You're the one behind this? The cops are looking at me like I'm guilty, and it was you all along?"

Maine ignored my outburst, instead turning his attention to Shahani. "I thought you told her?"

"I couldn't risk her having a fit like she is right now," Shahani replied, crossing her arms.

I stared between the two of them like they were bat shit crazy, which I honestly believed they were. "I'm not having a fit. I was dragged out of bed in the middle of the night to a warehouse where you have my husband tied up, ready to kill him with a machete. The fact that I'm still standing here is proof that I'm having an under reaction."

"Nubia, now both you and I know if Vincent had the opportunity, he would try to kill you again," Shahani countered. "You mean to tell me that you want this bastard roaming the streets, plotting and waiting for the perfect time to kill you? You must be out of your mind."

I yanked the handkerchief out of Vincent's mouth, wanting to hear what he had to say about Shahani's claims. "Nubia, you know I would never intentionally hurt you. Yes, we shared some heated words, but I didn't mean for shit to escalate the way it did. I love you, and all I wanted was for you to come home."

"Untie him," I said to Maine.

Maine chuckled at my request. "I told you what would happen if this nigga put his hands on you again, and I meant it. Shahani, move her back."

"Shahani, let go of me," I shouted, trying to move Shahani's grip on my arm, but she was too strong and had no trouble tugging me away from the impending blood bath. "Shahani, if you let this go down I will never forgive you!"

"You don't have to," she shot back, grabbing my other arm and restraining me so I couldn't get to Vincent, who Maine was circling like a hawk assessing its prey. "I'll thank myself every single night you're alive because this piece of trash is dead."

"Maine, please don't to this," I begged, fighting Shahani, who only held on tighter.

Maine dropped the machete on the tarp and stood still, studying Vincent, who despite knowing his life was on the line, refused to give Maine the satisfaction. Maine cocked his fist back and hit Vincent square in the jaw. I screamed at the resounding crack that echoed throughout the warehouse. The force of the punch knocked Vincent over, sending his head crashing into the ground. Maine dropped to his knees and continued to pummel Vincent.

"Maine, please stop it! You're going to kill him!" I shouted as Maine's blows grew stronger. Vincent coughed, and a small fountain of blood poured from his lips. "Maine, you can't kill him!"

Maine picked up his machete and lined it up with Vincent's neck. He raised it over his head and asked, "Give me one good reason why I can't?"

"Because..." I cried, sweaty, faint, and tired of holding this secret in for so long. "I'm pregnant."

Maine

I know she didn't just say what the fuck I think she just said. She didn't just tell me that after everything she been through with her husband, she was stupid enough to get pregnant by him. From the moment I met Nubia she has done nothing but sell herself short, thinking it was okay to be with this nigga, and the moment she figures out that love doesn't involve being someone's punching bag, she pulls this shit.

"And?" I said with a shrug. "No child should have to grow up watching their mother be beaten. You'll hate me now, but you'll thank me later."

"No, I'll always hate you if you do this, Maine," Nubia cried. I turned to face her and she was deadass serious. "He's the father of my child, and I can't stand here and watch you kill him. If you kill him, then you'll have to kill me too."

"Nubia—" her friend started.

I rose off the floor and stalked over to Nubia, whose chest was heaving as silent tears streamed down her cheeks. "If you take him out of this warehouse, I don't ever wanna see your ass again, you understand me?"

"Fine," Nubia said without meeting my eyes.

"You gon' keep fucking around with his ass and end up in a pine

22

box," I said matter-of-factly. "And before you get to blaming anyone, blame your motherfucking self. Now get this nigga outta my warehouse before my good graces run out and I kill him anyway."

I watched as Nubia untied Vincent and helped him to his feet. Even her homegirl didn't want to help her, and only stepped in because she saw Nubia struggling. She shot me an apologetic look on their way out of the warehouse. Shorty knew just like I did that this was a recipe for disaster. When she called me and explained why Nubia was avoiding me, I knew immediately that I needed to dead whatever she had with Vincent, and shorty agreed. She was the one that set me up with his known whereabouts, making it easier for me to track him down so I could handle my business. I could see it in her eyes that she wanted Vincent dead as much as I did, and Nubia's news blindsided her as well. It was one thing for her to suffer by her damn self, but to bring a child into this bullshit was downright selfish. I said what I meant about leaving her alone after this. I had demons of my own, and I refused to take on anyone else's.

******

"What the fuck are you doing here?" Jessica asked as she leaned against her apartment door. "I haven't heard from you in weeks, and you think you can just show up to my place in the middle of the night uninvited? I'm supposed to let you in for what? So we can catch up over milk and cookies?"

"Listen, I ain't come over here to argue with you, Jessica. If you want a show, I can give your ass a show right now and wake up everyone in this fucking complex," I said, the little bit of patience I had disappearing. "Am I coming in or not?"

Jessica moved aside, giving me enough space to slide in. Once inside, I made a beeline for the bathroom, stripping out of the clothes I wore at the warehouse and placing them in the trash bag I had in my pocket. I made a mental note to stock up on more hoodies and sweats over the weekend. That was my second to last "business suit" and I needed to restock in case I had to ride out on niggas again. I climbed inside of Jessica's compact shower and proceeded to rinse the day off of me. It started with me stopping by Estalita's place for some breakfast and a quick fuck session; by the afternoon, I was making moves with Jodeci, and right at the afternoon mark I hit up Vincent's shop. It had been a long time since I rode out and handled that many people, but once I got into my groove it felt just like yesterday. Now it was time to wash the day off and start over fresh. I toweled off and entered Jessica's room where she had a set of clothes laid out for me.

"You hungry?" she asked from her bed, where she sat sipping a mug of tea. Beside her was a plate of chicken and mac and cheese from KFC. "Had I known you were coming over tonight I would've made something."

She could front like she was mad about the time all she wanted; I would show up every night at the same time for the next month, and she would still answer the door for a nigga. Plus, she was talking out the side of her mouth if she wanted me to believe that she knew how to cook. I had been fucking with her for a little over a month and hadn't seen her do anything more than boil a pot of water. The longer I sat here, I asked myself why I ain't go to Niqua's house, where she made dinner every night, and even if she didn't, she had no problem cooking me up a three-course meal in the middle of the night. Jessica slipped out of bed wearing nothing but a black silk negligee, and I remembered why.

"Stop looking at my ass," she said as she flounced over to the trash bag I had placed on the floor, giving me a perfect view of her fat pussy.

I lay back in bed, enjoying the view as I finished off my food. "Trust me, that ain't what I'm looking at right now."

"Really, Maine?" she picked up the bag and glanced at me over her shoulder.

I shrugged. "What you expect a nigga to do when you over there looking all delicious, smelling like vanilla ice cream. Come over here and lemme lick you all over."

"Shut up," Jessica laughed. She shook the bag in her hand. "What do you want me to do with this?"

"Leave it there. I'll take it out in the morning."

She stared at me uncertainly. "Is there anything inside of it that I need to know about?"

"Depends," I finished off my last piece of chicken and held the plate out to her. "You ready to ride for a nigga, or you still married to this KFC shit?"

"I am not married to KFC. I stay there because the environment is better than the other places I've worked. Trust me, if I even smelled a better opportunity, I would turn in my shirt with the quickness," she said from the kitchen. She appeared in the doorway, watching me with those pretty eyes of hers. "If you want me to ride then say the word."

"It ain't that easy," I said, placing my arms behind my head. "You gotta prove yourself loyal before I let you in on a damn thing."

Jessica slipped out of both straps to her nightgown and let it fall to the floor, revealing her slim, but curvaceous frame. She was slim thick, which made it easy for me to manhandle her little ass, but I also got to appreciate that cushion when I dove in deep. Even though I loved her body, it was Jessica's eye contact that gave me a hard on every single time. She could see into your soul right before she sucked it out of you. Right now, they were locked on mine as she trailed my dick with her tongue and sucked it like a pro, proving that if she was half as devoted to me as she was to my dick, then there was no way she wouldn't be a benefit to the team.

"You like that?" she breathed, getting real nasty with it and allowing a stream of saliva to fall from her mouth and onto my dick.

She used it to wring my shit while focusing on the head. I grabbed the back of her head and fucked her mouth. One minute I was picturing Jessica, and suddenly she was Nubia riding me. I imagined her beautiful face contorting in ecstasy as I hit it.

"You like that?" I barked, biting my bottom lip as she picked up the pace, tightening her pussy to the point where I was seconds away from busting. "Huh?"

"Mmmmm..." she moaned, playing with her pussy. "Just like that, Daddy."

I reached out and grabbed her by her small waist and hit her with long strokes that had her screaming my name until she came all over my dick. I came right after her, busting one of the most intense nuts I ever felt. My eyes fluttered open and I was back in Jessica's bed. She sucked up every bit of my nut and swallowed it with a smile. I lay back in the pillow still in shock from the fantasy. First Nubia was popping up before I could get some pussy, and now she was intruding on my fuck sessions. Every time I thought I was done with this girl she crept back into my mind, making herself at home. I could've blocked her out and moved on with my life like I planned to, but that felt too easy.

"Bend over," I ordered a smug looking Jessica.

Jessica did as she was told and arched her back like a cat in heat. I slipped on a rubber and proceeded to fuck her like she was what my life had been missing, when in reality she wasn't. I missed the infuriating way Nubia barreled into my life with her stubborn ways, giving me all these feelings I didn't understand. I knew it was only a matter of time that circumstance brought us together again, and when it did, I hope she was ready to ride with a real one.

******

I spent the rest of the night wide awake, only slipping into a light slumber, when Jessica slipped out of bed to get ready for work. I took that as my cue to get up and get my day started. I needed to check in with Jodeci to make sure the numbers were right, and that niggas were getting the product on the streets in an efficient manner. Sampson mentioned that since I took over, sales had been up. He didn't have plans to be in the game forever, and with his son set up to take over Chicago, I knew it was only a matter of time before he would be looking for someone to take over, and my hungry ass would be ready. Speaking of hungry—

"*Buenos días,*" Estalita purred into the phone. "Are you busy, Jermaine?"

I glanced over at Jessica, who was sitting in the passenger seat, steadily typing on her phone. "I gotta make a quick drop, but I can come through."

"*Muy bien,*" she said, and hung up.

Jessica looked up from her phone and shot daggers at me. "Make a drop? Why couldn't you just tell the truth? That you were dropping your woman off?"

"I never said you were my woman," I replied matter-of-factly. "I don't hand that title out to every bitch I meet."

"Now I'm a bitch? I wasn't a bitch last night when I was sucking your dick."

"Because your fucking mouth was full," I shot back. "Every fucking time I think I might take you seriously, you come at me with some bullshit, Jessica. If you wanna become my main, you gotta learn how to think before you speak."

"Or maybe I have to be docile like Nubia to get your attention," she muttered under her breath.

"What?"

"I said maybe I need to act weak and pathetic like Nubia in order for you to take me seriously. Because it's looking like being a stupid bitch is the only way to get a nigga's attention nowadays."

I shook my head, not the least bit surprised that it came back to this. "How did the conversation go from you not knowing how to shut the fuck up, to Nubia?"

"Don't deflect, Maine. I saw the pictures of you and her leaving the club together. I'm sitting here giving you the best of me, and all you're giving back is some bullshit."

"Nah," I said, stealing a glance at her. "All you been giving me is high cholesterol and a headache."

Jessica unclicked her seatbelt. "Let me the fuck out."

"We're in the middle of—"

"I don't give a fuck what we're in the middle of, Maine. Let me out because I'm over you and your shit. I'm beautiful, I get money, my pussy is A1, and this is my real hair. Nubia will never see me on her best day! If you wanna keep your standards low, then by all means do you, but let me the fuck out because I'm tired of dealing with you and this back and forth."

I looked ahead to the highway I was speeding down, to Jessica, who had her arms crossed and was glaring straight ahead. With a jerk of my wheel, I crossed three lanes and parked on the side of the road. Jessica gathered her purse, jacket, and coffee mug, and climbed out of my car without a backwards glance. I sat there for a few seconds to give the appearance of giving a fuck, then gunned it into the morning traffic. I glanced in my rearview mirror and saw her chasing my car, waving her hands in the air like she was crazy. That would teach her to bluff with a nigga known for chasing everything but a bitch.

******

My stomach was on fire when I reached Estalita's. I wasn't in

29

the mood to fuck, but if she called me over this early in the morning she must've gotten into another argument with her father and wanted a shoulder to cry on. I would half listen to her Spanglish ramblings while busting down whatever she made for breakfast, then heading out. Or at least that was the plan until I was snatched off the street with a sack placed over my head. These cartel niggas fucked with the wrong one. I stuck my leg out behind one, tripping him and giving me the leverage to elbow the other one in the stomach. I had the sack halfway off of my face when I was struck in the back of the head, unconscious before I hit the ground. I woke to the smell of Mexican food, laughter, and the feeling that I was in the middle of some bullshit.

"Ah," Salvador Ordonez said as the black sack was pulled over my head. "It appears as if our visitor has awoken."

Salvador wasn't alone; his brothers, Fabio and Vincente, sat beside him on the plush leather sofa of the penthouse suite we were located in. A demure Estalita was sitting on his other side, wiping her eyes as she sobbed softly. One tug of my arms and legs told me there was no way in hell I would make it out of this chair alive if I didn't say the right things.

"Do you have any idea why I brought you here?" Salvador asked, his tone cool as he took in my disheveled appearance.

I stared him straight in the eye and replied, "I have no idea, but I can't say I'm anything more than honored to be in your presence, *jefe*."

"Nicely played," Salvador replied with a laugh that would've been considered humorous if it didn't bare his teeth like a rabid animal. "Lately, I have been having issues containing my daughter. You see, she has it in her head that she should be able to live on her own and see the world without a husband. Call me old fashioned if you must, but no daughter of mine will be allowed to leave my house unless she's moving into one with her husband. I told her as much, and you know what she told me?"

I shrugged my shoulders. "Nope."

"She told me that I wouldn't have to worry about that much longer because her *novio*, Jermaine, planned to take her away when his finances were in order. Is that what you promised my daughter?"

Shit. "Of course I promised Estalita that I would be with her when the time is right. She means the world to me, but like I said, a young lady coming from such a prestigious family deserves the best."

The brothers conferred with each other without taking their eyes off of me. Estalita beamed through her tears, mouthing a watery, "I love you." When they were finished, Salvador made a chopping motion with his hands, and I braced myself to be sliced and diced. However, it didn't come. One of his men cut the cords binding me to the chair, freeing my arms and legs.

"What if I can ensure that you're able to achieve such momentous heights sooner rather than later?" Salvador asked, admiring his pinky ring for a split second to intensify the look he gave me. "That while you have riches with Sampson, I can give you wealth."

"Sampson has been good to me since I can remember. He picked me up outta the streets when I was a kid—"

"I'm not asking you to leave him. Actually, I prefer that you still work for him for the time being. However, you must understand that if you are going to see yourself having any serious relationship with my daughter, then you must have your financial situation in order."

"You're absolutely right, which is why I accepted a promotion from Sampson so that I can give her the life she deserves," I replied.

Estalita leaned on her father's shoulder. "See, *Papí*. I told you that Jermaine takes our relationship seriously. He's been working harder so we can be together."

"I see, *mi hija*," Salvador replied without taking his eyes from mine. "Now he's going to have to put in some overtime."

Nubia

Although Maine had done quite the number on him visually, Vincent was still physically able to take care of himself. Once we were in the safety of Shahani's car, he literally held himself together. That slack jaw I saw back at the warehouse was the result of a broken jaw, which was probably the only reason why Vincent hadn't gone off on me; his mouth literally wouldn't let him. Shahani spent the entire ride to the hospital shaking her head as her gaze traveled between Vincent and me. She let him off at the corner of the hospital, refusing to get too close and risk having her plates read. I offered to take him to the emergency room entrance, only for both of them to object. Shahani pulled off without even checking to make sure he made it in, her reasoning being that if he didn't make it, he was likely to end up on the morning news. I didn't like her reasoning, but I didn't argue with it, and remained silent the rest of the ride home. She broke the silence first, waiting until she parked to get into my ass.

"You're pregnant," Shahani said incredulously as she stared at the ceiling of her car. "When did you find out?"

"When I was at the hospital. They ran a blood test and told me that while it was faint, they could detect the elevated levels of HGC. Once I missed my period this week, I used one of those dollar store tests you keep in your cabinet, and it came back positive." I leaned my head against the window, watching as parents walked their children to school. "This is something out of one of my worst nightmares."

"Are you going to keep it?"

I turned to look at Shahani like she had grown a third head. "Of course I'm keeping my child. They didn't ask to be born into this bullshit. I know you keep thinking it's a possibility, but I'm not going back to Vincent."

"I was asking because, if that's the case, then you need to be making money from now," Shahani replied. "I know I'm not a *wife* or anything, but whether I was married or not, I would want to bring my child into this world knowing I could take care of them, with or without a father."

"Which is why I'm going to come to work with you today so I can get my job back from Gordon."

"I already told you that I would—"

"No, *I'm* going to talk to him," I replied, placing a hand on my chest. "There's no more protecting me anymore. Now, *I* have to protect *us*."

Shahani didn't argue; if anything, she appeared to be a little proud. I was proud of myself as well. I let Vincent run my life for so long that it took having his in my hands for me to realize I couldn't depend on him any longer. Although I had no part of it, he would always blame me for his abduction and attempted murder. There would be bad blood between us forever, and I was going to have to do me in order to make sure my child had everything it needed. My parents died for me, and I would be damned if I didn't love my child that hard.

******

After getting only a few hours of sleep, I woke around three in the afternoon to the sound of Nia blasting Uncle Luke's "Scarred" while shaking her ass as she made lunch. Donovan sat at the table watching the show with mild interest. Not wanting to find myself in the middle of some mess that wasn't any of my business, I closed my eyes and woke up a little louder this time. Neither one of them changed what they were doing, so I guess there was nothing to hide. Shahani came out of her bedroom fully dressed in her work uniform, glanced between the two, and said nothing as she entered the kitchen. *Okay, so I obviously overthought this entire situation*, I thought as I climbed out of bed.

"Why didn't you wake me up?" I asked Shahani on my way to the bathroom to take a shower.

Shahani gave me an apologetic shrug. "You looked so peaceful; I didn't want to bother you."

The only reason I looked so peaceful was because it was the first night I slept knowing exactly where Vincent was. I had a feeling he wouldn't make another attempt to hurt me for a very long time. Maine had done a number on him, and now Francesca could nurse him back to health since she wanted him so bad. I told her as much when I called her to show up at the hospital. My last step in showing any interest in this situation would be to find out how long Vincent would be in the hospital, so I could know what necessary moves I had to make.

"You think shorty showed up at the hospital?" Shahani asked on the way to KFC. "I'm willing to bet $20 that she packed her shit and left."

"Nah, she's his 'true love.' Trust me when I say she'll be around for a hot minute. One look at Vincent lying in that hospital bed looking like shit, and she'll melt."

We discussed the situation from Miami, and I opened up to Shahani about the threesome. She squeezed her steering wheel so tight that her hands were nearly white. I could see her jaw working, and prayed she wasn't thinking of doing something crazy, like showing up at the hospital to finish what she started. After a few minutes of deep breathing, she hugged me tight and promised me that everything would be all right.

"You're gonna go in here, sell Gordon your best self, and handle business for my little niece or nephew, understand?" Shahani said.

I followed Shahani's directions to the tee, walking into the restaurant with my head held high and a smile on my face. It faltered when I spotted Clifford, the area coach, but I wouldn't let him intimidate me the way he used to. Shahani noticed the faltering in my steps and gave me a gentle nudge. Clifford, Gordon, and Jessica were sharing a laugh next to the sandwich station when I showed up. The smile Jessica wore dropped when she laid eyes on me. Clifford noticed the exchange, but remained silent on it.

"Gordon, you and I spoke earlier this week on you interviewing Nubia, and here she is," Shahani said and bowed out gracefully, giving me my chance to have myself heard.

"What's your schedule looking like, Nubia?" Gordon asked, picking up his clipboard and pen.

"I can be here whenever you need me," I said with a shrug.

"Straight closing if you want."

"What size shirt are you again?"

I opened my mouth to reply when Clifford cut me off. "Gordon, didn't you already hire that girl I sent here yesterday?"

"I did but—"

"Then I think you should slow down on the hiring, especially with hours getting tight," Clifford replied, relaying an unknown message with his eyes that Gordon didn't receive until he looked at his boss.

"Oh, so because Jessica doesn't like me, I don't get to work here?" I said, feeling my temper rise. "That pussy must be real good if you got this lazy bitch telling you how to run shit, Clifford."

"Excuse me?" Clifford growled.

I shrugged my shoulders. "You're excused. I came in here looking for a job with no problems or trouble, like I have been from when I worked here. Now you wanna curve me getting hired because she said so?"

"You been walking around here scared to have an opinion, and now that you have one, you wanna direct it at me?" Jessica said, taking a few calculated steps towards me. "Bitch, I'm not your fucking husband; when I put my hands on you, I'mma break your fucking face permanently."

I snapped. I don't know if it was because she called me out of my name, or because of the remarks she made concerning my relationship with Vincent, but one minute I was standing there listening to her talk shit, and the next Shahani was pulling me away from Jessica as Gordon pulled at my hands. Clifford was shouting for me to let go of Jessica, who was screaming as she tried to land a few blows of her own, but I was deflecting them like it was second nature. Sadly, it was. My anger got the best of me as I let go and gave her one final kick in the chest, knocking her and Clifford back into the cash registers.

"When I see you again, bitch, I'm fucking you up on sight!" Jessica screeched at the top of her lungs.

"Not if I see you first, bitch!" I shouted back as Shahani dragged me out of the kitchen.

"Nubia, have you lost your mind!" she shouted once we were in the parking lot. "I brought you here to get a job and you go ham on a bitch! And to top it all off, you're pregnant!"

I crossed my arms and shrugged, unapologetic. "Once I caught that shade from her, I knew two things: Gordon wasn't gonna hire me, and I could take that bitch because all she has is mouth. So I went for it, because at this point I ain't got shit to lose, now do I?"

"I guess not," Shahani said with a hint of a smile. "And you did get that bitch real good. You see how she was screaming before she started trying to fight you?"

"Sure did. She only started getting bold when she saw Gordon holding my hands. No, bitch, back up all that shit you was just talking. I beat you the way my nigga used to beat me, and I bet that'll be the last time you talk some shit to my face."

Shahani playfully punched me in the arm and promised, "When I get home, we are going to do a big ass job hunt, okay? Plus, Donovan has a bunch of connections all over Brooklyn. I'm sure we can have you set up somewhere real nice by the end of next week."

I watched as Shahani entered the restaurant to start work, and all the confidence I had seconds ago disappeared. Both she and I knew there was no way in hell I would be able to find work somewhere else with my face looking like this and a small ass resume that only had one job on it. I was in a fucked up situation that would have me on the welfare line if I didn't get my shit together. I walked away from the restaurant, refusing to have Jessica or any of its inhabitants see me crying. The tears increased and the streets grew too blurry to navigate this late at night. I was swiping at them when I bumped into someone.

"I'm so sorry—"

"Nubia?"

I wiped my eyes and saw Mitchell standing in front of me looking concerned. He must've been on his way to work. "Hey, Mitchell. Sorry for running into you like that. I had some stuff on my mind and—"

"What's going on with you? I heard from some people that once you left KFC your husband started putting his hands on you? That's what you're crying about?"

"No...I...uh...I just got into this big ass fight with Jessica, and now I know I can't get my job back. It was mainly my fault. It felt good at first, but now I'm starting to feel stupid. I've got priorities and business to handle with no hopes of having a job come through."

Mitchell scratched the back of his neck. "I may have a job you can do a few days a week if you really need the money. I'mma be honest though—it ain't a legal gig."

"How illegal are we talking?" I asked, my expression unsure.

"All you gotta do is deliver a few packages a week. Nothing serious," he replied, pulling out his phone. "Lemme get your number and I'll hit you with some more details."

I gave Mitchell my number and he promised to get back to me with some more details at the end of the night. After getting myself together enough to be around the public again, I hopped on the bus and arrived back at Shahani's place. Everyone was out, presumably getting money, except for me. I snuggled into bed and by the time Mitchell called me, I was ready to do whatever it took to secure my bag and my child's future.

******

I stood in line at the print shop scratching at my sweaty palms. It had been ten minutes since they called another person, and I was growing impatient. I tried my best not to look at the surveillance cameras, but I snuck a peek anyway and felt my heart hammering against the strap of the backpack I was wearing. After making the line full of impatient customers wait another five minutes, another representative came to the front and began taking customers. The line sped up and I finally made it to the front. I slipped her the receipt Mitchell had given me and waited patiently as she gave me a medium sized package. I placed it in my messenger bag and with a curt nod, entered back into the crisp fall afternoon. I was so tense that the ringing of my phone in my pocket scared the shit out of me.

"Did you get the package?" Mitchell asked once I picked up the disposable cellphone he gave me last week.

"Yeah, I'm on my way with it right now." I started down the street to the car where Precious sat waiting for me. "We should be there within the next hour."

"Good. You remember what you're supposed to say when you get there, right?"

I nodded even though he couldn't see me. "Special delivery."

"Good. I'll have my niggas looking out for you."

Precious was in the car bumping trap music as she filed her pointed nails. According to Mitchell, she got into being a courier in order to pay for her own nail salon. She had been doing runs for the past few months, and her aloof attitude easily cancelled out my nerves. One look at the sheen of sweat on my forehead had her laughing out loud. She handed me a napkin and pulled off.

"Girl, you act like this is some serious shit. I mean it is, but the way Mitchell and his boys got this down pat makes it too easy. We pull up to the spot, you hand him the package, take the money, and we drop it off to Mitchell. I've been doing this for a minute and ain't had no trouble yet."

"Really?" I said, checking her expression to make sure she wasn't lying to me. "You haven't been pulled over, followed, nothing like that?"

"No. My man used to have me do runs for him before he got locked up. Don't worry—it had nothing to do with the runs. It was for some other bullshit he got caught up in dealing with one of his friends. He's getting out soon, and I wanna have my shop set up so we can get our cash flow back to what it used to be."

"I'm trying to do the same for myself. I found out that I was pregnant a couple weeks ago, and my husband ain't shit. I can't go back to being his punching bag. He won't give me any money, so I'm out here making sure I'm set up for my baby when the time comes."

"Trust me: you do enough of these runs and you will be. In a good month I can make—shit! Here we fucking go!"

Police lights came on behind us, followed by a microphone stating, "Pull over."

"I cannot believe this bullshit," Precious muttered under her breath as she puled over. "Nubia, you better calm the fuck down and don't say shit, you understand me? I got this."

I checked my rearview mirror and saw that not only was it the police, but it was detectives. They probably watched me from when I came out of the print shop and followed us. I fucked up, and now I was going to jail for the rest of my life. *How can she sit there looking so damn calm,* I thought as I watched Precious sit up straight with her hands on ten and two. She was dressed smartly in a pair of chinos with a chambray shirt, looking more like a Gap employee than anything.

Precious rolled down her window and politely greeted the detective with a bubbly, "Good evening, Officer."

A bright light flashed in my eyes as the detective's partner flashed his lights on the interior of the car and me. I almost forgot to breathe for a moment, and the whoosh of air I exhaled caught the attention of the detective, causing him to flash his light on me.

"Are you aware of why I pulled you over?" he asked, returning his attention back to Precious, who was still cool despite the interruption of our plans.

Precious shook her head. "I have no idea."

"Where are you on your way to?"

"My friend and I are on our way to a function with some friends. I may have been speeding just a little because she has to use the bathroom."

The detective ignored her response and said, "License and registration."

Precious handed over the necessary items and watched as he went back to the car. His partner stayed and made sure to let us know we were still being watched by keeping his flashlight trained to the ground.

"Please tell me your license and this car is clean," I muttered under my breath. "Precious…"

Precious didn't say anything; she stared straight ahead and drummed her hands on the steering wheel. I knew there was but so much I could say out the side of my mouth without causing attention and settled with remaining quiet. The detective returned after a few minutes, and I just knew he was going to let us go with a warning.

"Ma'am, I need you to step out of the vehicle."

"Excuse me?" Precious exclaimed. "My tags and license are clean—"

"Ma'am, I need you to step out of the car. Now!"

The detective on my side knocked on my window, and I knew what that meant. I stepped out of the car, careful to leave the messenger bag on the seat. I was cuffed and placed on the curb with Precious, who was seething. She stared straight ahead, her jaw working as she took controlled breaths. The detectives combed the car, and I felt my heart leap into my throat when the detective came out with the box from my bag. He gave it a little shake and walked over to me.

"What's in the box?" he asked, his eyes boring into mine.

"It's a package I'm picking up for my grandmother," I lied. "I have no idea what's inside of it."

"Where'd you pick it up at?"

"The place where you pick up packages," I replied as if it was the simplest answer in the world.

"What's inside of it?"

"I have no idea, Officer. She told me to pick up her package, and I did what I was told to do."

"Well, I detect a funny smell coming from it, and I'm going to open it," the officer replied, whipping out a box cutter and slicing the tape down the middle of the box. He opened it and looked inside, a large smile growing on his face. "Look at what we got here…"

The other detective came over and looked inside of the box. Both of the men shared a laugh with each other. Precious' face was a mask of anger, and she refused to acknowledge either man while I wanted to see what the fuck was so funny. I was on my way to prison for the rest of my life; I might as well have a good laugh on my way there.

"You wanna see what it is?" the detective asked, giving the box a little shake.

I shrugged.

He tilted the box in my direction and showed me the three white bricks. I found nothing funny about looking at enough cocaine to send me to jail for the rest of my life. It wasn't until I took a closer look that I realized that it wasn't cocaine. It was—

"Sugar?" I said incredulously.

"Congratulations," the detective said with a chuckle. "You passed the test."

"Test?" Precious and I exclaimed.

We were uncuffed and helped to our feet by the now friendly detectives. The one that pulled us over said, "You did a good job. The grandmother thing was smart. Next time, don't be afraid to make eye contact. Have a good night and send Mitchell my regards."

I was handed back my box and watched as the men slipped into their car and drove away. From this view, nothing about their car or attire screamed undercover, leaving me to wonder whether or not they were even detectives to begin with. On one hand, it was great because that meant there was some sort of protection. On the other, it meant that if their hands weren't oiled well enough, we could end up in prison for the rest of our lives. All in all, it told me that I needed to find a new job ASAP.

"*D*amn, you can't keep spoiling a nigga like this," Vaughn said, but that didn't stop him from opening his mouth for another bite of the lasagna I was feeding him. "Where you learn how to cook?"

"My mother was a stay-at-home mom, so I learned how to get down in the kitchen from her," I said, and it was partially true; whenever Nichelle would cook she always told me to get the fuck out of the kitchen, as if she was making sure I couldn't become her competition later on. I learned, though, by watching from around the corner and making a mental note of everything she used. "She taught me everything she knows."

"I hope you ain't including that trick with your tongue," Vaughn replied in between bites.

Nichelle was especially responsible for teaching me that tongue trick, and as of right now, it still got me whatever I wanted from a nigga. The only legacy that bitch passed down to both of her daughters was how to be the best hoe you can be. From a young age my older sister, Paris, and I were sat in front of our mother and taught how to properly service a man. Once we turned twelve, it was time to put those lessons to work. Paris had been getting it in with niggas for a whole year, and I watched enviously as she was given the finest clothing and jewelry that money could buy. For someone with everything I ever wanted, she was always walking around looking sad and stressed. She ended up running away and marrying this construction worker that had to be at least ten years older than her. I thought it was crazy considering how she had the attention of every hot nigga on the block, but with her gone, there was more attention for me. And attention was what got me kicked out of Nichelle's house and had me hustling from a young age. But now, I was getting ready to cash out with Vaughn.

"You don't need to know where I learned that from; just know you're the only one I use it on," I purred as I fed him another bite.

We went on like this until I was finished feeding him, and then it was time for me to put Vaughn to bed. I rubbed his belly until I felt like his food had digested and literally fucked him to sleep. Instead of focusing on my own pleasure, the greatest nut I had came from satisfying a man like Vaughn that could get me whatever I wanted. He wasn't in the streets too deep, but I knew he had to be doing something to afford this nice spot in the heart of Bed Stuy. I had done some apartment shopping in this area, and there was no way you could afford the rent unless you had a roommate, which wasn't the case for Vaughn; between his moans and my screams, someone would've been showed their ass. Especially when I walked around with all of my ass out, giving him a show while I cooked and cleaned.

"Why can't you stay the night?" Vaughn asked after our intense fuck session.

I pecked his neck. "I already told you; I gotta work late tonight."

"Man, I already told you to quit that job," he murmured, running his hands through my hair. "I'll take care of you."

I placed my chin on his chest, getting a good look at him to figure out whether he was serious, or if it was the pussy and full stomach talking. "We haven't been fucking around long enough for me to let you finance my life."

"Well, then how about I put some money in your pocket?"

"As nice as that sounds, I prefer working for my money," which was the full truth; after getting my ass beat by Sly, I learned that there ain't a better feeling in this world than having your own so a nigga can't go upside your head because he "made you."

"I got a job for you then. I'm shooting my music video tomorrow, and I want you to be the principle girl. The pay was a stack, but since you my girl, I'mma hit you off with five."

Five thousand dollars to be cute and show a little body? That was right up my alley. "What time do you need me to be there, baby?"

"You gotta be there early for hair and makeup since we'll be shooting all day. So about six, seven in the morning. I'll have a car pick you up in the morning." I was halfway out of bed when he asked, "Where's my kiss at?"

I leaned over and locked lips with him, making it nice and sloppy the way he liked it. I had to bite my lip to keep the cheesy smile on my face from spreading. I had dealt with my fair share of street niggas, but none of them were like Vaughn. He was so passionate that I found myself entertaining weird shit I wasn't used to, like cuddling and together time. My last nigga would slap the shit out of me if I had the nerve to ask him for a cuddle, let alone some attention. I was still in it for the money—that would always be my main goal—but there was something about Vaughn that made me smile. I was still smiling when I got home. It wiped off my face when I saw Donovan sitting at the table waiting for me.

"Where the fuck you been?" Donovan asked in a voice barely above a whisper.

I continued to my room without stopping and shot over my shoulder, "I was out."

"Out with who!" Donovan was hot on my heels, and I didn't know whether or not Shahani was home from work yet.

I glanced over my shoulder at Nubia, who was sound asleep on the couch. "Donovan, calm down before you wake her up!"

"She ain't woke up none of the nights I been digging in ya guts," Donovan shot back as he shoved me into my bedroom and closed the door behind him. "I don't think a mature conversation between two adults will wake her."

"There's nothing mature with you putting your hands on me," I shot back, the words tumbling past my lips before I could stop them.

Donovan slapped me across the face, sending me crashing back onto my bed. "Watch how the fuck you talk to me. I'm not none of these lil' niggas you been fucking with. I treat you right, don't I?" I nodded. "Then treat me with the respect I deserve."

"Yes, Daddy," I said, remembering that I wasn't back with Vaughn. "I'm sorry, Daddy; that won't happen again."

"It better not. Now tell me where you been?"

It was rare that Donovan repeated a question, and I knew better than to give him a bullshit answer for the sake of saving face. I chose the truth, and prayed that I wouldn't regret it. "I was out with this guy I met."

"You giving my pussy away?" I stared down at the comforter for a split second before Donovan yanked my face up to meet his. "Don't look down. You wasn't acting this humble when you was fucking another nigga, so don't play coy now. Who the fuck is this nigga you been giving my pussy away to?"

"He's a rapper named Butta."

Donovan cracked up, a healthy laugh escaping his lips. "You out here fucking a nigga named Butta? I can't believe this shit…"

"He's a big deal, Donovan. You can Google him and see what he's about. He offered me a role in his music video tomorrow."

"How much does it pay?" Donovan asked with no preamble.

"Five stacks."

Donovan ruffled my hair like a proud father, his hand massaging my scalp and warming me up. "So you wasn't out there just giving my shit away. Why didn't you say that in the first place?"

"I…I thought you might be mad because I was fucking with him," I stammered, leaning into his hand as it traveled to my cheek. "I didn't wanna tell you until I had secured the bag."

"Well you did, and Daddy's proud of you," he said, biting his lip as he stared down affectionately at me.

He pissed me off ninety percent of the time, but I had a soft spot for Donovan. Maybe because he was the first man to come into my life that gave a fuck about me more than my own father did, wherever his bitch ass was. Sure it might look like we only had pimping in common, but he always gave me the guidance I needed and got me into line when I stepped out. Some might consider it rough, but love was never supposed to be easy.

"Yo, what you doing?" he asked as I reached out and pulled down his gray sweats and boxers. "Your cousin will be home any minute now."

"Oh please, it ain't like we haven't fucked while she was home," I said, recalling the time we were getting it in when she walked through the door from work. Donovan had to sneak back out the house and shower at his boy's house next door so she wouldn't become suspicious. "Besides, isn't that part of the thrill?"

The relationship between Donovan and I wasn't something that came overnight, but that didn't make it small by any means. However, a big part of it was sneaking around to keep Shahani from growing suspicious. Donovan still needed her help to reign the girls in until I got the hang of running shit. Then I would take over, and she would be given her walking papers. It wasn't like Shahani would care anyway; I had been watching the subtle changes in my cousin, and I had a feeling she was fucking around with Sampson. I showed up at KFC a couple times looking for her, and she wasn't there, which eased any guilt I felt for fucking her live-in boyfriend.

"Damn, Nia," Donovan hissed as I deep-throated him. I smiled up at his closed eyes and the look of ecstasy on his face as I snatched a piece of his soul from him. My tongue swirled the tip of his dick as I massaged that sensitive patch underneath his balls, and he started speaking in tongues. "Shhh-fuuu-got damn."

Donovan got to vibrating and not even a minute later, I was swallowing his kids. He collapsed on the bed beside me, spent from what had to be an intense orgasm. With Nubia around, our fucks became far and few, with us only being able to get it in on the nights Shahani closed, or when I was doing outcalls and Donovan got a room for us. I placed his dick back in his sweats and laid on his stomach, enjoying the companionable silence until I heard the clicking of the lock on the front door. I listened as Shahani dropped her stuff off in her room and made her way to mine. I had barely cleared the other side of my bed when Shahani turned the knob and let herself in.

"Nia, have you seen—Donovan, I was looking for you. You're not going out tonight?" Shahani asked with mild interest. "I got a text from Puddin' saying that she had some terms change with her client, and she needed you to come and pick her up."

Donovan sat up slowly, shaking his head. "I already explained to that nigga that my girls ain't into that BDSM shit. Tryna use them up and run trains on them for a couple stacks. These bitches bodies be fucked up, they don't need their minds gone either…"

He rose from the bed and left the room without a backwards glance, his mind on autopilot when it came to making money. Shahani watched him leave the room with mild interest. I thought she would follow him out the room and help him get ready, but she chose to stay behind. She closed the door behind her and stood against it, watching me with those alert eyes of hers. If I thought being raised by my mother was fucked up, then what was Shahani's life? The system forced her to grow up fast, making her street literate before she was fully literate. I had a good poker face, but Shahani always had the upper hand. All it would take was for her to talk with me for five minutes to find out everything she wanted to know.

"You know, if you don't want Donovan crashing in here, you can tell his ass to get out," she said. "I know he thinks he runs everything, but your room is off limits."

I waved away her concern. "He was asking me where I was because he thought I was working tonight. I told him I wasn't because I was too busy spending time with my new nigga."

"Who is this new guy? I hope he's nothing like the other ones you dealt with in the past."

I shook my head vigorously. "Nope. He's a sweetheart and he's also paid. He's this rapper named Butta."

"I think I've heard a few of his songs before. 'I Stay Strapped' featuring Carter?"

"Yesss!" I said doing a little dance.

Shahani and I talked for a few more minutes, and it felt like old times where we would chill at her place in the city. Her old boyfriend, Alonzo, kept her in this beautiful penthouse suite in the city, and she would invite me over every weekend to keep me from hanging in the hood. Those were some of the best times in my life, and Lonzo was something like a brother to me. He was one of the few respectable men I ever had the pleasure to meet. I remember one time he caught me walking around in my panties while Shahani was out and gave me a long lecture about loving myself and wearing pants whenever I was in his house. I did love myself, but I wanted a taste of him at the same time. He never held it against me though. Those were good times, and I wondered what happened to her tonight for her to want to come and talk to me.

"I know with everything going on I haven't been the most attentive cousin to you," Shahani said, opening the door. "But I'm gonna work on improving that, okay?"

I nodded. "I'd like that."

"'Night, Nia."

"'Night, Shahani."

The smile I wore slid off my face. I don't know whether or not I eased her suspicions, but I knew it was no coincidence that she came to shoot the shit with me. Maybe she was hoping she would guilt me into leaving Donovan alone, but I guess she didn't know that little Nia was replaced with a big, bitter bitch that would do whatever the fuck she wanted. If I could fuck her man in her house, then I could easily fuck her feelings in her face.

Simple as that.

******

The video set was popping when I arrived, with everyone in a bright and cheery mood despite the fact that the sun had only risen an hour ago. I was by no means a morning person, but when I saw the huge buffet table with mountains of breakfast food, I knew a waffle or two would put me in a better place. I had barely filled my plate when I was whisked to the makeup chair. The artist was one that I followed on Instagram, so I knew she would beat the hell out of my face. Suddenly, this entire situation felt a little more real, and I didn't have an appetite any longer. My face was finished, and I was in the middle of being styled when Vaughn and his crew showed up. Hoes started coming out the woodworks, calling out to him and walking by in the smallest of swimsuits to catch his attention. I was nothing short of impressed when Vaughn kept his gaze trained on me.

"Good morning," I purred, smiling from ear-to-ear when Vaughn pulled me in for a hug. I saw Jodeci watch the hug with a knowing look on his face, before heading for the buffet. "Damn, you showed up looking delectable. Got hoes popping up calling your name. What do you have planned for these groupie bitches today?"

"They're for the strip club scene," Vaughn replied, taking a seat in the makeup chair and allowing the artist to start on him. "We made sure to get this spot up here so once I'm done shooting with you, I can head downstairs to the strip club."

"I like, I like," I said as the stylist placed different outfits to me and asked for my approval. To Vaughn I asked, "So, what's this song about?"

"It's about me giving up on chasing hoes and settling down with a special woman that I can build with."

I placed a playful finger to my chin. "I've seen the hoes flock to you, but you've always been tied to your girlfriend, Drea. Shouldn't she be here right now instead of me?"

See, while everyone thought I was bullshitting about Butta being my favorite rapper, I was deadass serious. I followed all of his underground music, and Sly took me to all of his events, which was why I knew he had a serious girlfriend since everyone could remember. Drea made herself known at every event and was all over his social media. I had been itching to find out what their relationship status was, but didn't want to ask until I was sure that Vaughn was feeling me. Turns out I was right for playing patient.

"Drea and I are taking a break from each other right now," Vaughn said with a nonchalant shrug. "She felt like she could do better without a nigga, so I'm letting her."

I always knew in my heart of hearts that bitch was crazy. There was no way I would ever let a faithful ass nigga like Vaughn out of my sight. He curved females on the regular for her, and now he was doing the same for me. Unlike Drea's ungrateful ass, I planned on riding this entire situation until the wheels fell off. When it came time to get in front of that camera, I became the woman that Butta had been chasing his entire life. We shot throughout the luxury suite, spending time in the kitchen, to "making love" with the view of New York City behind us. Our last scene was of me lying in bed, giving the camera a perfect view of my body drenched in silk sheets, as Butta got ready to hit the streets to hustle. By the time I was done, everyone had to be thinking, *Drea who?*

That is, until she showed up on set making a big scene.

"Yo, who let her up here?" Vaughn shouted from the makeup chair. He was getting ready for his scene downstairs at the strip club, and I was keeping him company. "Drea, the last time I spoke to you, you made yourself perfectly clear that you wasn't fucking with me anymore. So you need to get the fuck off my set before I have security drag ya' ass out."

After being together for damn near twenty years, that's how you're gonna treat me?" Drea shot back. One of the security guards placed a hand on her shoulder, which she swatted and growled, "Don't put your fucking hands on me."

"Drea!" Vaughn barked, and I was instantly introduced to another side of him I had never seen. "If you wanna talk, we can talk later on, but right now you're showing your ass in front of my company, and that ain't cool."

Drea's eyes rested on me, and I knew by the deep frown on her face this wasn't her first time seeing me. Shorty must've got an eyeful of me on Vaughn's IG when he was tagging me and liking my posts. "So this is the hoe you plan on replacing me with? Vaughn, you can't be serious right now."

Plenty of other bitches would've gotten up in arms about being called out of their name, but not me; call me whatever the fuck you want, but I bet you can't call me broke. I could tell that she was looking for feedback from me and was disappointed when I didn't even pay her ass dust, simply pulling out my phone and texting my homegirl, Essence. She was one of Donovan's girls, and we had become close over the past couple of months. A message from Donovan popped up as well, asking me for the location to the set, which I studiously ignored; there was no way in hell his ass would come here to ruin my good time.

"First you walk up in my shit making a scene, and now you wanna talk shit about my girl." Vaughn snapped his fingers. "Brooks, get her the fuck outta here."

Drea broke down crying, her pretty face contorted in pain. I watched her drop to the floor sobbing, mildly impressed by her ability to go from mad to sad in 0.5 seconds. When having a tantrum didn't work, she resorted to bawling her eyes out. There was no way in hell someone could spend twenty minutes, let alone twenty years, with me and watch me cry on the floor, which was why I knew Vaughn was fighting everything in his being to comfort Drea.

"How about this? Since I'm done shooting, I'll head out and let you get your situation handled," I said, sliding out of my chair and grabbing my purse.

Vaughn gave my hand a gentle squeeze. "Good looking."

We stood at the same time and went into separate directions, with me making a break for the side door as Vaughn went to comfort Drea. Everyone was looking at me with a newfound respect, Jodeci included.

"Lemme walk you downstairs," he said, following behind me.

I didn't know much about him, other than the fact that he was deep in the streets. He was full of jokes and stayed playing when I hung with him and Vaughn at the club, but there was always this alertness behind his eyes that told me he wasn't someone to be played with. Like right now, as we stood waiting for the elevator. The doors pinged open and we stepped on, standing shoulder to shoulder.

"You know they're gonna end up back together, right?" he asked, staring down at me as he waited for my reply.

I stared back with a bright smile, disarming his hating ass. "I like Vaughn. A lot. And even if I can't be his woman, then I have no problem being his friend. That's how hard I fuck with him."

Jodeci pulled an envelope out of his pocket and held it out to me. "Here's your pay for the day." I closed my fingers around it and gave a sharp tug when he didn't let it go. "I can double that if you agree to stay away from my boy."

"Fine, I'll stay away from him. Now where's my money?"

"In the envelope; I knew a greedy hoe like you would never turn down some extra money," Jodeci said, shaking his head in disgust.

The elevator doors pinged open, and I wasted no time stepping out of the elevator and leaving his bitch ass alone. Yes, I agreed to stay away from Vaughn, but if he was half as sprung over my pussy as I thought, there was no doubt in my mind that he would be coming to me. I chuckled all the way home, still giggling when I walked through the door. Nubia was nowhere in sight, but the house was clean. *She must be out at that new job of hers*, I thought, noticing that her jacket and purse were gone. I made a beeline for the bathroom, wanting to scrub the day off. I had succeeded and entered my bedroom dripping wet, to find Donovan lying in my bed.

"So I spent most of the morning on that nigga's IG, watching him pretend to fuck the shit outta you," Donovan said coolly. "Is that the reason why you been ignoring all of my calls?"

"I wasn't ignoring any of your calls, Donovan. They didn't allow me to have my phone on the set," I said, grabbing a towel and lightly patting the excess water off my body so I could oil myself down.

Donovan climbed off the bed and rolled up on my like he was getting ready to beat my ass. I cringed when he put his phone so close to my face my nose flattened. It was a video of Vaughn and I watching

59

Drea have her nervous breakdown. I was engrossed in my phone at the same time Donovan sent me a message. He moved his phone and stared at me, his expression unchanging. I could feel the heat radiating from him and knew I was going to pay for lying to him.

"You still wanna claim you weren't ignoring me?"

Silence.

"You ain't got shit to say because you fucked up."

I bit my lip, contemplating on pulling a Drea and breaking down in tears, but a pimp like Donovan was hip to theatrics. All I could do at this point was shoot straight with him. "I fucked up and I'm sorry."

"It's too late for sorry. Get your shit and get the fuck outta my house," Donovan said, backing up and making his way to the door.

I expected him to fly off the handle and maybe manhandle me a little, but never would I have expected for him to kick me out. I had the money from the video shoot, but I wasn't trying to move out long before I was ready. And I wasn't ready to end my relationship with Donovan either.

I flung myself at his feet and wrapped my arms around one of his legs. "Donovan, please don't be like that. You know I'm only fucking with this nigga for a come up. I even managed to finesse his friend out of some extra cash, too."

"How much?"

"Five stacks. It's yours, baby."

After a few minutes of contemplation, Donovan said, "Get up off the floor." I scrambled to my feet and waited for the verdict. "We supposed to be in this together, Nia. The last thing I want is to feel like when a new nigga comes along flashing some bread, your loyalty to me will be swayed. I don't know what you're used to, but all my bitches hold me down, and I can call every last one of them and get an answer when I call."

"It won't happen again, Daddy. I promise," I said, tearing up at the thought of losing one of the most stable relationships I'd ever had.

"Good." Donovan moved to leave and I stopped him again, this time with a gentle tug that pressed his lips against mine. "Yo, I gotta handle some business."

"Your business will still be there when I'm done," I said between kisses. "Now come lay down and let me take care of you."

I went back into video vixen mode for Donovan, worshipping every part of his body. He loved it when I took special care of him, and right now I honestly didn't give a fuck who knew what we had going on. Our relationship might not have been perfect, but it wasn't for everyone to understand.

Shahani

I swear these hoes were liable to bring my blood pressure up to the point of no return. It was bad enough that I closed last night and had to come right back to open because of Jessica's scary ass, but now they were bringing themselves to my place of employment and making it look hot. Essence and Pinky stood at the counter, smiling and carrying on with the cashier on shift, a young girl named Rochelle. They were selling her a dream and I'll be damned if she wasn't eating it up, talking about how she needed extra money for her classes. I sent her little misguided ass to make coleslaw and had to keep from going upside her head.

"What the fuck are the two of you doing here?" I hissed, looking around to make sure the cook wasn't paying me any attention.

Essence spoke up, twirling her hair around her finger. "We came to see you because we haven't been able to get in contact with Donovan for our pay."

"What do you mean Donovan hasn't been paying you? He's been leaving the house to handle business all this week. How have you not seen him?"

"We just haven't," Essence said with a shrug. "Can you ask him tonight for us? Our landlord can only take threesomes but so many times before his wife starts asking questions."

62

"I'll get in contact with Donovan and have him get with you. Is that all?"

"No, we'd like two $5 Fill Up Boxes," Essence chirped. "I've been out working all night and I'm starving."

Pinky cosigned with a nod, but I could tell that something else was bothering her. I asked her what was going on when Essence went outside to have a smoke while the biscuits were baking.

"It's none of my business," she said, glancing nervously over her shoulder. "But I think I know the reason why we haven't been able to get Donovan."

"What?"

"No…forget it. I'm tripping…" she said, dismissing the thought.

I placed a comforting hand on hers. "You know deep down that you aren't tripping. You can tell me, and I promise it won't get back to Donovan."

"I think he's fucking Nia," Pinky blurted out.

I bristled at her admission. "Girl, what?"

"They've been spending a lot of time together—"

"Because he's my boyfriend and she's my cousin. He's looking out for her," I shot back, suddenly on the defensive. Pinky looked frightened by my outburst, and I knew I had to calm her down before Essence came back in. "I'm sorry, I ain't even mean to come at you like that, you just caught me off guard. I know you may think you're seeing something between the two of them, but trust me: ain't nothing going on."

"You're right," Pinky said, though I could tell that she didn't fully believe it.

Essence returned and the awkward moment was gone as fast as it came. I sent them on their way with complimentary meals and went back to work. Although I would never admit it to any of my girls, I had my suspicions about Nia and Donovan. I guess with me being wrapped up in my affair with Sampson, I rarely paid any attention to what was going on inside of my house. I came home, took a hot shower, went to sleep, and did the same thing over and over again depending on the day. Today was no different, with me taking a detour on the way home that led me to Sampson's Long Island lair. I made sure to have Mitchell cover for me just in case anyone stopped by, which gave me ample time to spend out there with no worry of Donovan, Nia, or anyone else calling down my phone.

"Wassup," Sampson said, greeting me at the front door with a kiss on the lips and a light slap on the ass. "I drew a bath for you and laid out something extra nice for you to relax in."

"Is that your way of telling me that I stink?" I joked as I slipped out of my shoes and padded across the heated marble floors.

"No," Sampson said, drawing out the word as he led me upstairs. "That's my way of letting you know that you need to relax when you come here. Whatever bullshit you got going on with your nigga, dead that shit at the door."

While Sampson's ten bedroom, six bathroom mansion had everything a girl could ask for—a movie theater, gym, an indoor and outdoor swimming pool, and a kitchen stocked with everything you could ever want—my favorite place to be was the bathroom and the bed, in that order. Sampson used these expensive vanilla and almond oils to draw me a bath and rubbed my body down when I was done. It always pained me to have to wash it off when I got home, but Donovan had the nose of a bloodhound, and any foreign smell to him was a red flag. But right now, I would enjoy my time to be treated like royalty.

"What's wrong with you?" Sampson asked as he rubbed whipped Shea butter onto my legs, those strong hands of his making sure to work out any minor kinks. "You've been quiet since you got here."

"One of my girls told me that she thinks Donovan is cheating on me with my cousin," I admitted.

"Why would you care?"

I bristled at his remark. "Why would I care? Because he's my boyfriend and she's my cousin."

"And you're sitting here cheating on him without a conscience," Sampson countered, his hands traveling up my legs and paying special attention to my kneecaps.

I placed my hands on top of his, stopping him so he could pay attention to me. "Who said I didn't have a conscience? You think I'm here fucking you and going home to him like it's nothing?"

"You come back. Every other day. You must not feel as bad as you claim, or else you would stop playing games and make a choice. Now it looks like the choice is being made for you, and you're still acting like that's where you wanna be."

"He's fucking MY COUSIN!!!"

"AND WHAT DO YOU EXPECT FROM A NIGGA THAT SOLD YOU?!!!" Sampson roared, chilling me to my core. In a cold tone, he said, "If by that nigga's side is where you wanna be, then get the fuck out of my house, and don't come back."

I slapped his hands away from me and stalked over to the closet where I kept my clothes. "Trust, you ain't gotta worry about ever seeing me—ouch!"

Something hidden in the white shag carpeting dug into my foot. I reached down and dug my hands around a little, gasping when I saw what it was. So Sampson was sitting here acting like I was fucked up, when it was obvious that he was entertaining other bitches at his house.

"I guess I'm not the only one fucking somebody else," I said, holding up the expensive diamond earring. "And it's not a cheap hoe either."

"Don't worry about what the fuck I'm doing because I've given you ample times to shut the shit you got going on with your boyfriend down, and you refuse to. Did I have a bitch here? Yes, I did. But what the fuck do you expect me to do when you go home to your nigga every night?" Sampson waited for my reply, but he had me stumped and he knew it. "That's what the fuck I thought. Now get your shit and leave."

I dressed hastily, hoping to at least clear the foyer before the tears started to fall. I had my main nigga fucking around with my cousin, and my side just broke up with me. This was too much to handle in one day, and all I wanted to do was go home and forget that today ever happened. Sampson followed me downstairs, silent though his presence was anything but. I refused to look back at him and give him the satisfaction of seeing me this fucked up. The large door slammed behind me, leaving me out in the cold.

"Calm down, Shahani, calm down," I said to myself on the drive home.

I kept the mantra going until I was parked in front of my house, where the dam broke and the water works erupted. How did one night of passion become an affair, and even if Sampson and I were only fucking, why did it hurt for him to tell me it was over between us? Because I loved him. Because the time we spent in Chicago consisted of some of my most positive memories in recent memory. Then why was it so fucking hard to let go of what I had with Donovan? Because he was the first man to show me love after I stopped believing I was deserving of it. I was torn between contentment and possibility, and it was tearing my heart apart.

"You know what? The only way I'm gonna be able to deal with this situation is if I go up there and ask him," I said, wiping my eyes and applying a little light makeup so he wouldn't notice I had been crying. "If he's honest, then we can work through this and become better."

I did a light jog up the steps, bracing myself for one of the hardest conversations I would have in my life. I guess I didn't brace myself hard enough because once I entered my apartment, I heard the sound of slapping skin and fucking. Nubia was knocked out on the couch, still dressed in her street clothes, her hand resting lightly over her stomach. I crept deeper into the apartment and recalled the same fucking noises being made one night I came home from seeing Sampson. Last night when Donovan was lying on Nia's bed looking like he was high, had me thinking it was because he just got finished taking a hit of her pussy. I cracked the door open a peek and decided that the next hit either one of them got would be with Mercy. I slid her out of my purse and quietly opened Nia's bedroom door.

"Say it again," Donovan barked as he plowed into Nia from behind, slapping her ass so hard it rippled. "Say it the fuck again!"

"I'm sorry, Daddy!" Nia moaned, tossing it back to him. She had tears in her eyes, and I wondered what kind of exchange they had before I came home. "I promise I'll never put another nigga before you!"

Another nigga? So lemme get this straight. My cousin was fucking my nigga and had the nerve to have a side nigga of her own? Instead of keeping the man she had, she chose to dump him in order to keep fucking with mine? No. This was too fucking much. I kicked the door open like SWAT and charged at Nia, grabbing her by the hair and giving her a good old taste of Mercy in action. Like the little bitch she was, she started crying and screaming. The commotion caused Donovan to lose his balance and go crashing to the floor. He rebounded quickly and started prying us apart.

"Shahani, let her go!" Donovan roared, eating some of the hits I dealt to the openly crying Nia.

Nubia appeared in the doorway, rubbing her eyes as if to make sure what she was witnessing was real. She jumped in, grabbing my hands and whispering in my ear, "Shahani, let go of her. It ain't even worth it! You're better than this!"

My grip on Nia's hair slackened for a split second, giving Donovan the chance to push me off of Nia. Nubia and I tumbled into dressers, knocking over perfumes and lotions. I picked up a heavy Burberry perfume bottle and lobbed it at Nia, cracking her right in the forehead.

"Yo, what the fuck is wrong with you?" Donovan barked, grabbing his jeans from the floor and jumping into them.

I let out a peal of laughter at the blatant audacity of this nigga. "What the fuck is wrong with me? You're fucking my cousin in my fucking house!" I leapt and tried to grip up a still sobbing Nia, only for Donovan to intercept me. "And you, bitch! I took you into my home, gave you a job, and you repay me by fucking my man? Donovan won't be here to protect you forever, bitch! You see this gun in my hand? On God, I'mma show you what my bitch can really do. You just wait and see."

"Shut the fuck up, Shahani!" Nia shouted, gaining a little courage because I was still wresting with Donovan to let me go. "Don't sit here and try to act all perfect like you ain't been fucking around too! I've went to KFC plenty of times looking for you, and you ain't been nowhere to be found. I'm willing to bet everything I own you been fucking with Sampson."

Donovan stopped fighting and looked down at me. "Is that true?"

I shrugged out of his grip. "Yes, it's fucking true. And I've been going to bed almost every night feeling guilty for fucking around on you, when you been getting it in with my cousin!"

"How long?" Donovan asked calmly. When I didn't answer quick enough he shouted, "HOW FUCKING LONG!"

"Since you set it up the first time," I cried, poking him in the chest. "You promised me that no matter what happened, I would never become one of your hoes, and you broke that promise. I don't give a fuck whether or not I forgave you for it, you still put me out there like that!"

"I know." Donovan chuckled at the shocked expression on my face. "I know you been fucking Sampson, and that's why I've been fucking your cousin! Getting all up in her guts. Turning her into the real bitch I thought you were. Now I realize I should've left your disloyal ass on the pole I found you on."

"You should have, because maybe I'd be something by now! Oh, you think this was my dream? I've been with you for six years and you've yet to show me something real. No ring, no real commitment, no nothing but a bunch of hoes that won't even have viable pussies by 2020! Fuck you, Donovan. Fuck you and that raggedy ass bitch. I hope you catch whatever her hoe ass has."

"Don't mistake me for you, bitch! That old nigga probably gave you worms," Nia barked, curling up in the tangle of sheets and reaching for her phone. "Fucking bitch gave me a knot on my head. How am I supposed to get any work with this knot on my head…"

"Damn, Nia," Nubia said as she followed me out of the room. "Everything she's done for you and you mess with her man? That's low, even for you."

"You wanna hear about low?" Nia said, and I could tell she was getting ready to spit some cold shit to Nubia.

I stopped at the door and hissed, "Nia, leave her the fuck outta this."

"No, she wants to hop in the middle of something that doesn't involve her, lemme let her know that being a hoe runs in the motherfucking family."

I turned around and gave her a pleading look. "Nia…if you open up your mouth and say what I think you're about to say, you're dead to me."

"Shahani, what is she talking about?"

"Nothi—"

"You don't ever wonder why Shahani doesn't like Vincent?" Nia asked matter-of-factly. "Why Vincent was at KFC the day you met him?"

"What does that have to do with Shahani?" Nubia said, her eyes growing shiny.

"He was there because she was fucking him." Nia let out a hearty chuckle at the shock and hurt on Nubia's face. "And they were fucking well into your relationship, too. Why'd you stop fucking him, Shahani? Did he drop your lame ass for Nubia, or did that 'conscience' you claim to have finally kick in?"

Nubia turned around and stood there, waiting for me to confirm or deny. When I did neither, she knew what was up. "You were fucking him?"

"Nubia, it wasn't anything serious. I—" She tried to step around me to leave the room, but I couldn't let her until she heard me out. "Nubia, please listen to me!"

"I don't wanna listen to a word you have to say! Now move out of my way before I move you!"

I stepped aside and let an openly sobbing Nubia get by me. She cried as she picked up her duffle bag and shrugged into her coat. I approached her, begging for her to hear me out and listen to my reasoning for why I never came clean with her on the relationship Vincent and I shared.

"I don't give a fuck, Shahani. You smiled in my face, knowing that I was dating a nigga you were actively fucking. Then when shit went left with the two of you, all of a sudden you're telling me that I need to leave him alone? Why?" She shrugged her book bag on her shoulder. "Have you known he was always this abusive?"

"Yes, but I never thought he would put his hands on you," I said, hanging my head in shame. "The only reason I knew was because…I'm sorry Nubia."

"I'm sorry for ever thinking you were my friend," Nubia said, brushing past me and walking out the door.

I plopped down on the couch, shaking with silent tears as the only victim in this entire situation got hurt the worst. Donovan appeared, hands in his pocket, laughing at the sight. I looked up at him thinking he would at least grow ashamed and leave, but that was too much to expect from this trash ass nigga.

"Looks like all of that hoeing caught up to your simple ass, didn't it?" he said, grinning like a Cheshire cat. "I want you out of my apartment now. Take everything you came with and leave."

"You can have all of this shit!" I screamed, flipping the coffee table over, sending magazines, and candy flying everywhere. "I don't need it, and I don't need you."

"Make sure you leave the keys to my whip on your way out. I can give it to someone more appreciative," Donovan said as Nia appeared by his side, wearing nothing but a grin.

I took the keys out of my pocket and sauntered over to the couple, holding them out with an air of impatience. Donovan snatched them out of my hand and gave them to Nia. I looked her in the eye and said, "The same way you get a man is how you'll lose him. When everything starts to crumble and he shows you his true colors, I hope you're ready to handle it. Because I won't be here. Bitch, you're dead to me."

I took one last look at my apartment and for the second time tonight, left with my head hung. I had nothing but the clothes on my back and the extra money Sampson had given me after the first night we shared. Sitting on my stoop, I broke down crying at how my entire life had been snatched away from me. I wasn't sure how long I had been sitting there when someone tapped me on my shoulder. I looked up and there was a familiar face.

"Come with me," he said, holding out his leather glove clad hand.

I accepted it and was placed into the backseat of the Cadillac Escalade parked curbside. The heated seats got to work on me, and I was knocked out halfway to my destination. I was woken up by the backseat door opening and the crisp air blowing across me. My eyes fluttered open and the chauffer from my trip to Chicago stood there waiting to help me from the SUV. I stepped out and made my way up the walk. Three doorbell rings later, the door opened, and I was engulfed by warmth mingled with the smell of roasted chicken. Sampson stood there, watching me with that cool gaze of his as I tried to find the right words. I opened my mouth and a sob came out, scaring me. He opened his arms wide and I walked right into them, the familiarity enough to sooth me. It took a lot of time and bullshit, but I knew where I wanted to be, and was happy to belong there.

Nubia

Three months later...

I stared down at my phone, watching as it rung nonstop like it did everyday at noon for the past three months. She could call until she was blue in the face. I had no time for Shahani and whatever excuses she might have. Once I walked out of her apartment, I was on my own with very few options in sight. I didn't have any family, and Shahani was my only friend, which left me calling Precious to see if I could stay with her for a few nights. As it turned out, her roommate moved out abruptly, leaving her with an extra room. I moved right in and had been putting half on the rent ever since. Everything was chill, I was making money, and my little nugget was doing just fine.

"You need to answer that bitch's call so you can move on with your life," Precious said, staring at my phone with contempt. "Or better yet, throw the whole damn phone away and get you something from this decade."

I placed my Assurance phone in my purse and stuck my tongue out at her. "I'mma tell you like I tell everybody else: ain't nothing wrong with my phone. It's free and does everything I need it to."

"Yeah, except in six more months you're gonna need it to take pictures of this little angel," Precious replied, reaching over and giving my belly a little rub. "How many months are you?"

"I'm four," I said with a hint of pride. "I find out what I'm having at my doctor's appointment next week."

"It looks like you'll be having a girl to me," Precious said, studying my slightly protruding belly. "That's exactly how my stomach looked when I had Marlee."

"Where is Marlee's little behind at?" I said, looking around for Precious' precocious four-year-old daughter. "She's been awful quiet."

Precious waved her hand dismissively. "That girl is back there watching one of those princess shows and steadily adding to the tab for her birthday. So far, I'm already spending three G's and you know her bitch ass daddy ain't putting shit in on it. That nigga got out of jail and said fuck me and my baby. I really lucked out when I met Paco, or else I don't know how I would've been getting my rent paid."

Paco was Precious' new boyfriend, and if he was an upgrade like she claimed, then I didn't even wanna know what her old boo, Sullivan, was about. Paco had to be one of the wildest thugs I had ever seen in my life, and Precious ate him and all his crazy shit up. His wild eyes found their way to me every so often, and I thought telling him that I was pregnant would deter him. Instead he was always telling Precious that she needed to get pregnant because "pregnant pussy is the best," which had me ducking his deranged ass every chance that I got.

"I feel you girl," I cosigned.

Precious checked her watch. "Aren't you supposed to be going on a run today?"

"That's not for another hour or so. Mitchell said this package was a little heavier than most, so he didn't want me out at high noon gaining too much attention."

"Ooh, okay girl. Which spot is he having you go to?"

"The one over there on Broadway, and I'm taking it to Dro at his spot."

"Damn," Precious exclaimed, placing her hand on her chest. "He wants you to bike all that way with your belly?"

I waved away any concerns she might have. "I spoke to the doctor and she said it's perfectly fine for me to bicycle as long as I take breaks." I felt my phone vibrating in my pocket, and I knew it could only be one person. "Really, Shahani? She's calling me back again. It must be something serious. Lemme call her back."

I went into my bedroom and called Shahani back, pacing the floor as I waited for her to answer. She picked up on the second ring and sounded genuinely surprised to hear from me. All the anger I felt for her betrayal wilted, and I was tempted to make up with her on the spot and put everything in the past, but then I thought about how if Nia would've never blown her spot up, she would've still been lying to my face.

"Nubia," she said, sounding relieved to hear my voice. "How are you? Where are you? Is everything okay? How's the baby?"

"I'm fine and so is my child," I said curtly, taking a seat at the edge of my bed and playing with the thread in my blanket.

"That's good to hear. Do you need anything? I now you just started working when we last—"

"I don't need anything from you, Shahani," I cut her off. "I got it.

All this time you were absolutely right about me; I depend on others too damn much. Well not anymore. I might not have my shit together all the way, but it's together enough for me to not need anything from someone who smiled in my face for years, and fucked my man behind my back. Were you helping me because you were guilty?"

"Of course not!" Shahani choked out. "Nubia, you are like a sister to me. I tried telling you that Vincent was no good but...but I didn't wanna hurt you."

"Well you hurt me anyway! You could've also saved me a world of hurt by being upfront with me, but I guess that was too much to ask for from someone that claims you're like a sister to them. What else are you hiding, Shahani? What's the reason why the two of you broke up?"

"Nubia..."

"Are you going to tell me or not?"

"How about I tell you in person?"

"How about when you're ready to tell me without the dramatics, you give me a call back? But for now, stay off my damn line," I said, hanging up on her and laying back in my bed.

Just when I thought maybe we could build a bridge and try and start over with our friendship, Shahani started back with that secretive shit. I was over it, and so pissed, that I took a nap. The front door slamming followed by Paco's loud ass woke me up. I checked the time and saw that I had an hour to get where I needed to be. I grabbed my winter coat, messenger bag, and the ten-speed bike I bought at Wal-Mart, and headed out. Paco and Precious were sitting on the couch enjoying dinner as I passed by.

"Girl, I made you a plate," Precious said, motioning to her own plate of steak and mashed potatoes. "You don't wanna sit with us and eat before you go?"

"No," I said, studiously ignoring the way Paco was licking his lips at me. "I'll eat later on."

"Suit yourself. Be safe out there," I heard her say as the apartment door closed.

The January air was frigid as I rode through the busy Brooklyn streets, looking out for black ice and any other obstacles that could send me skidding into oncoming traffic. The ride gave me something to focus my mind on aside from the situation with Shahani. While she was fucked up for hiding this situation from me, she wasn't the only one I was mad at. I tried reaching out to Vincent for some type of financial assistance, and only ended up cussing him out on his voicemail. I tried again the next day and his phone was out of service. I was really raising this baby on my own, and the only thing keeping us alive was the hustle.

"Wassup, Nunu," the print shop clerk said as he passed me a package. "Make sure when you're done at the other spot you make a stop at the wash and fold, aight?"

"Got you," I said, knowing I would be paid at the wash and fold. "See you around."

I had memorized the route from the check-cashing place to the spot where I make my drop by now. The sun had already set, and I knew the darkness would be the perfect cover for me. I plugged my headphones into the little cheap MP3 player I bought from Fat Albert and jammed out to the radio. I could see the building ahead, shining like a beacon, and had zoned in on it when I was tackled and knocked onto the sidewalk. The down from my coat cushioned the blow, with my head barely touching the pavement. I bounced back quickly, bolting upright and into the barrel of a .45. I place my hands in the air and stared right into the eyes of my robber.

"Listen, I don't want any problems," I said, pleading with the masked stranger. "But I can't let you take this package without knowing the consequences. This belongs to some important people and if you take it they'll come looking for you."

"No, you stupid bitch, them niggas coming looking for you. Now gimme the fucking package," the gunman barked, digging the barrel into my forehead.

I pulled the crumpled package out of my bag and held it out, jumping when it was snatched from my hands. I thought the gunman would leave me alone after that, but I guess having my life literally in his hands wasn't enough. He raised his gun and cracked me in the face, knocking me into a realm of darkness.

******

I woke to the sound of crying, sobbing that could only happen in the depths of your heart. Like trying to scratch a pain in your heart that wouldn't go away. Or when you got caught up in some shit and your life was on the line. My eyes fluttered open, my lashes brushing against the cold cement floor of the warehouse I was trapped in. I groaned at the soreness radiating from my shoulder sockets from my arms being tied roughly behind my back. I saw shoes, a few pairs, and two people kneeling in front of me. I blinked a few times, making sure I was seeing things right. Kneeling in front of me was Precious and Paco. Both were dressed in hoodies, but Paco's looked real familiar.

It was the same hoodie of the person that set me up.

"Look who finally decided to join us," an amused voice said amongst the men. "Sit her up."

I was roughly placed onto my knees. Now that I was right side up, I could see who was who and wasn't the least bit surprised to see Mitchell, Jodeci, and a few other choice niggas standing there watching the scene. Jodeci snapped his fingers and one of the guys came over and removed the bandana from my mouth, along with Precious and Paco's. The bandana had barely moved from her lips when Precious started running her mouth at a mile a minute, begging them to hear her out.

"Mitchell, you been knowing me for how many years now? You know I would never do something like this to hurt the family. I was at home with my baby girl when all of this went down." Precious continued yammering on until Jodeci grew impatient.

He took three calculated steps to her and slapped her across the face, causing her to keel over. Paco watched with mild interest, his expression unchanging. I took deep calming breaths to keep from ending up like Precious. I had a child coming, and if I was blessed to make it out of this alive, I didn't want him or her damaged by this.

"You speak when you're fucking spoken to," Jodeci barked, and gone was the funny guy persona I had once given him. His cold eyes set on me, and he cracked a smile that looked more like a sneer. "Look at who we got here. Nubia Morris. Mitchell told me he hired a new girl to handle business for us, and you're honestly the last person I expected to run into. What happened, Nubia?"

I recounted my travel from the pickup to the drop off. Jodeci listened to my story, his expression softening slightly as I went through each and every single detail, leaving nothing out. Precious' sobbing fucked with my nerves a little, but I drowned her out and told my story. When I was done he walked away, nodding his head as he absorbed the relevant facts.

"Nubia, the only person who knew that drop was happening tonight was me, my employee that works at the print shop, and the person you were supposed to make the drop to. The only person who's looking guilty right now is you, because it's your people that got caught with my shit."

I closed my eyes, trying to come up with a valid explanation for why Precious and her boyfriend knew where I would be tonight. "I told Precious the route earlier today. She offered me a ride and I declined."

"Is that right…" Jodeci said, staring deep into my eyes for the truth. "So you had nothing to do with this?"

"Jodeci, if something was to pop off, I would be the first person y'all came looking for. Why would I put myself or my child's life in danger for whatever you have in that box? Both you and I know I don't have enough connections to flip product. Even if I did, everyone would know where it came from and you'd still trace it back to me."

"But Precious has those connections?" Jodeci asked, baiting me into turning on Precious, who had stopped crying long enough to hear what I had to say.

"I don't know. All I know is that I told Precious the location I was going to, and I was robbed."

"Did you know that Precious and her boyfriend used to dead niggas on their packs? This ain't her first ride around the rodeo," Jodeci said, reaching on his waist and pulling out a Glock. "Ma was gon' set you up for the missing pack and run off with this nigga right here."

"That's not true," Precious cried, attempting to shake her head against the tarp her and Paco were on. "Nubia, he's lying. I wouldn't do you like that. But I need you to tell them I ain't have anything to do with this. Please. Marlee is in the car sleeping. What is she gonna do when she wakes up and her momma isn't here anymore?"

"You should've thought about that before you decided to steal from me, bitch," Jodeci said, popping off two shots.

They whizzed past Precious and hit Paco, one in the neck and the other in the head. He hit the tarp with a thud, choking on his blood for five minutes before finally growing still. Precious screamed and cried for Jodeci to hear her out and listen to what she had to say.

"Paco made me do it," she admitted. "It was all his idea, Jodeci. I told him it was a bad idea, but he had it in his head that we could take the coke and start over in Maryland where his people could flip it. No matter how bad of an idea I told him it was, he wouldn't listen to me."

Jodeci mulled over her admission for a minute, and studied her the way he had done me only minutes ago, except this time there was something different about the look in his eyes.

"You got any last words you want me to pass on to your daughter?" Jodeci asked patiently.

"Jodeci, please," Precious begged, her sobs bouncing off of the warehouse walls. "Please don't do this to my little girl."

Jodeci really looked like he was considering letting her go, until his arm swung upward and he popped off two shots, hitting Precious in the head and killing her instantly. "Should've thought of that before fucking with my money. Get these two motherfuckers off the floor and get rid of 'em. Untie her."

I looked at the spot on my chest that he pointed to. "You're not gonna kill me?"

"No, my boy saw the entire exchange outside. They left you laying out in the cold. He spotted Precious' car from down the way and had someone grab her at a red light."

Mitchell came behind me and untied me, rubbing my wrists as he helped me to my feet. I flexed them as I watched Jodeci's men wrap up Precious and Paco like they were yesterday's trash. Jodeci studied me, following my gaze to the bodies and resting his eyes back on me. I knew what he was thinking and eased his worries.

"You don't have to worry about me saying anything," I said, crossing my heart and kissing my hand up to God. "As far as I'm concerned, Precious and Paco left in the dead of night."

"So then why did she leave her daughter?" Jodeci replied, asking for obvious reasons. "If you ain't got a good enough excuse, I'mma have to go over to that car and put a bullet in baby girl."

"I'll go to the police tomorrow morning and tell them I was babysitting for Precious last night, and she still hasn't come home. They'll look for Paco before they come looking for you."

Jodeci nudged his head at the car where I could see a slumbering Marlee, the lighting from her iPad illuminating her precious face. "You think you can get baby girl to go along with that?"

"Yes," I promised, nodding my head vigorously. "Then I'll get her to her father and you won't have to worry about her ever again."

"Make it happen," was all Jodeci said as he walked off. "Mitchell, get them out of here."

The ride home had to be one of the worst in my life, with Marlee snoring peacefully in the backseat, unknowing how much her world had changed while she was asleep. Every time Mitchell opened his mouth to talk to me, I gave him the hand, not in the mood for any of his apologies or explanations. It was only when I had Marlee safely back home and tucked into bed, did I finally confront him quietly in the living room.

"Ain't no need to whisper; they drugged baby girl when they picked up Precious and Paco. You might get lucky and she'll think everything that happened was a dream," Mitchell said, taking a seat on the edge of the couch. "Come and take a seat so we can talk about this."

"There's nothing for us to talk about, Mitchell," I said, hugging myself to keep from losing my mind. "They had me on the floor ready to put a bullet in my head, and you think I wanna talk? I wanna go to sleep and pretend that this never happened, but I can't. Because if I can't get that sweet, little girl to go along with my story, then they'll kill her and me, too."

"I wouldn't let anything happen to you, Nubia."

"You almost let Jodeci kill me."

Mitchell waved away the accusation. "He wasn't gon' kill you. I

85

vouched for you, but he needed to know that you were down. Now that he sees you ain't a snitch, you don't have to worry about something like that happening again. You'll be set up with someone more reliable and—"

"Set up with someone more reliable? Mitchell, I don't wanna see you or any of those…those thugs ever again. I'm done with this shit!"

"And how will you pay your bills, huh? How do you plan on feeding little Marlee until you find her father?" Mitchell posed each question as he pushed up on me, taking my chin into his hand. "You need this job, Nubia. Ain't no getting around that. You couldn't hold your own at KFC, you cut off Shahani, and your husband is posted up all over social media with his new bitch. Your only option is to keep working with me or live out on the streets. What happened last night is the bad side of the game, but can you really say your life hasn't benefitted from the good?"

"I'll find a way," I said, moving my face. "I don't care what I have to do, I'm not putting myself in danger like that again."

Mitchell laughed, a hearty chuckle that disappeared in a split second. He grabbed me by the throat and said, "I was trying to make you feel like it was an option, but it's not. You still got a package to deliver tomorrow. Your bike will be here in the morning, and if I'm in a good mood, I'll have an Uber parked out front."

"No," I said with a little more bass in my voice. "You don't run me. As a matter-of-fact, you don't run shit. I said I want out and I'm gonna stay out."

"I might have brought you in, but the only way you getting out is if you ask for permission from my employer."

"Make the appointment. Call whoever you need to call to get me out of this situation."

Mitchell made the call, and thirty minutes later, Maine appeared. Our tiny apartment was filled to the capacity with soldiers, some posting up by the windows as others stood guard at the door. Maine's eyes flickered to my slightly protruding stomach and back at me, his expression unchanging. I folded my arms, hoping it would take the attention away from it, when all it did was make it stick out even more.

"You wanted a meeting?" Maine said, mimicking my stance.

I dropped my eyes and saw Maine's hand twitch as if he wanted to reach out and lift my head, but the presence of everyone stopped him. I pulled my own head up and faced him head on, taking a few deep breaths before I started my speech.

"I—I—I've been handling packages for you for the past few months, and I want out. You don't have to worry about my loyalty; I know how to keep my mouth shut," I said, hoping Maine caught the double meaning in my words. "Please let me go."

Maine stared at me long and hard, those cold eyes of his taking in my wrinkled clothes, messed up hair, growing stomach, and the desperate look in my eyes. When he spoke it was with that same disinterest he shared when we first met.

"Mitchell, find somebody else to make the drops. Leave the girl alone. She's out," he said, making a move for the door, which created a ripple effect. "Let Jodeci know. I got some business downtown to handle for the rest of the night."

"Thank you, Maine," I choked out, holding my neck to keep that aching feeling at bay.

Maine turned around, and when he looked at me there was nothing welcoming in his eyes. "I ain't do it for you; I did it for your kid. It hasn't even made it out the womb and doesn't stand a chance."

His words stung, and burned once I was left standing in the living room by myself. Maine had saved me more times than I had saved myself, and it hurt to know that the one person that once believed in me, viewed me as a burden. This would be the last time I needed his saving; my back was officially against the wall, and I had no one to help me. Failure wasn't an option, and it was time for me to make the best of what I had.

Maine

The lights to my TriBeCa penthouse came on the moment I stepped off the elevator. Estalita sat on the couch wearing a sheer black kimono with a matching teddy underneath. Her long, toned legs were crossed, with the higher one bobbing up and down as she sipped on a martini. I could feel the argument brewing in the air and braced myself for it. Two more steps and there she was, on her feet storming behind me as I made my way into the bedroom, undressing along the way. Her Spanish diatribe was delivered to my back, bouncing off the bathroom walls and deafening me until I went to step into the shower. She blocked me and dropped to her knees. I was gearing up for some welcome home head when she had the nerve to start juggling my balls in her hand.

"What the fuck are you doing?" I barked at her, watching as she examined my dick under the bright lighting.

Estalita furrowed her brows at me. "What does it look like I'm doing? Making sure that while you were out that you haven't been fucking around with any *putas*. One of my *chicas* told me that I could measure your *cajones* before and after you left the house, to make sure you haven't ejaculated while you were out working."

"Since you're down there weighing them, you might as well smell them too," I said sarcastically. She leaned in to smell my balls when I punched the shower door behind her, giving her the fright she deserved. "I think your *chicas* forgot to mention that the only way for you to know if they're lighter, was if you weighed them in the morning before I left. Which you didn't."

Estalita clamored to her feet and stormed off, presumably to pout in bed. I would handle her ass in a minute, but for right now, I needed to wash off the day and rid myself of this excess tension. As hot jets of water from the six showerheads pounded my body, working out kinks in places I couldn't even reach, I did a mental rundown of my day. Ever since I had taken on the new territory given to me by the Ordonez Brothers, I went from making a modest living, to bringing in more cash than I would ever be able to spend. I started off every morning checking on my multiple businesses I invested in, the afternoons working in Brooklyn for Sampson, and my nights were mine to do what I pleased, which left me in the company of Niqua or whichever girl at my strip club caught my eye for the night. I came home to Estalita when I was done having fun and gave her the attention she claimed she craved until she knocked out. Normally, it was simple to keep her placated, but tonight, after seeing a very pregnant Nubia, my nerves were shot and all I wanted was some time to think.

"All he does is run the streets and I don't know what to do about it," I heard Estalita on the phone crying to one of her friends. "I know he's seeing other bitches, I just can't prove it. But when I do, I promise to tell my—Jermaine!" she barked angrily when I snatched her phone out of her hand and hung up on her friend.

I silenced her protests with a kiss, which she returned as she ran her hands hungrily down my damp body and snatched my towel off with one flick of her wrist. Estalita wanted reassurance that I wasn't going anywhere, and I gave it to her with the only language we were fluent in: sex. I stripped her out of the negligee she wore and hungrily devoured each part of her perfect body.

"Jermaine," Estalita whimpered as I dove deep with stroke after stroke. "Promise me I'm the only one."

I ran my hand through her hair and whispered the sweetest lie. "You're the only one."

Estalita came from those words alone, snuggling in my arms and forgetting about her accusations for the time being. I made sure she was sound asleep before slipping out of bed and making a beeline for the guest bedroom. I knew I could get four, five hours tops of sleep until I had to be back in bed with Estalita. I didn't trust my night terrors not to come back with the reentrance of Nubia into my life. She brought out the worst in me, which was once the best I had to offer. I knew I had to stay far away from her, but life had a knack of bringing us close together. Like right now, as images of her danced on the back of my lids as I slipped into a dreamless sleep.

******

I woke to a feather-light touch tickling my shoulder. The slight touch was enough to wake my entire body at once. My hand acted before my body, reaching out and grabbing the culprit as my eyes sought out the target. Estalita yelped and I let go of her, praying I hadn't hurt her. If she felt some type of way she didn't say a word, most likely chocking it up to being the reaction that came with my title.

"Your phone has been ringing off the hook," she said, holding it out to me. "Why are you asleep in here, Jermaine?"

I ignored her question and instead answered the call from Jodeci before it went to voicemail. "It's four in the morning. This better be about some real serious shit for you to be waking me out of my sleep."

"It is about something serious: who the fuck told you to give orders concerning my employees?"

"What the fuck are you talking about?"

"I got a call from Mitchell saying that you had a meeting with one of my employees and let them go."

I closed my eyes and ran a hand over my face; I can't believe this nigga was tryna pull a power play at four in the morning. "Where the fuck you at?"

"At my usual spot."

Thirty minutes later, I pulled up to Jodeci's building. Niggas were posted up out front and had the nerve to look at me like they wanted problems. I made eye contact with each of them soft mufuckas, staring straight into their soul and letting them know I'll snatch that shit from their body, and they sobered up instantly. I may have been splitting my time between two territories, but that didn't mean that I was to be disrespected, and I would let Jodeci know as much when I saw his ass.

"Hey, Maine," Rosa, Jodeci's moms, purred as she stood in the doorway. "What brings you by this early in the morning?"

"I need to speak with Jodeci. Is he here?" I asked politely, though the sound of NBA 2K18 and clouds of weed smoke let me know that

Jodeci was here.

Rosa ran her hand down the front of my Mackage coat and replied, "This is a really nice coat. What kind of material is this?"

I was saved from having to continue the awkward conversation that would lead to a proposition, by Jodeci shouting, "Ma, who is that at the door?"

Rosa rolled her eyes and swung the door open. "It's Maine."

Jodeci was sitting in the middle of his soldiers engrossed in the video game, barely holding on to the blunt perched between his lips. He made a point and half the room cheered, while the other half dismissed their excitement with the wave of a hand. There was no way in hell I left my place in the middle of the night to sit here and watch these niggas play a fucking video game. I unplugged the PlayStation 4, which caused a moment of uproar until they saw who pulled the plug. The only person bold enough to challenge me was Jodeci, who was on his feet in an instant.

"Yo, what the fuck is your problem coming into my spot and disrespecting my shit?" he barked, motioning to the television.

I cocked my head to the side and shot back, "Nigga, you disrespected my sleep and you thought I was gon' roll the fuck over and act like nothing happened? You wanted to talk business and now you got the opportunity to speak your fucking peace." I motioned to all these niggas sitting here watching with bated breath. "Rise the fuck up outta here so we can talk."

They were halfway to their feet when Jodeci stopped them. "These ain't your soldiers to tell when to move."

I took a step closer and replied, "I tell you when to move. So if I said get the fuck up and get the fuck outta here so we can talk, I mean GET THE FUCK UP AND GET THE FUCK OUT SO I CAN HANDLE MY FUCKING BUSINESS!"

Everyone scrambled to their feet and headed out the front door with a mention that they would be downstairs. Jodeci cut his eyes at their hasty departure and back to me, his chest heaving. Ever since I was given territory by the Ordonez Brothers, Jodeci had been gunning for my position as lieutenant, being that it was only a matter of time before I was running shit over there full-time. He went from being my fun loving brother to my competition. He was constantly trying to one up me and our friendship was starting to suffer for it. I had been ignoring his actions as of late, but tonight was the last straw. Whichever one of these niggas that got into his ear and told him it was aight to call me and question my authority, needed to be dealt with.

"Where the fuck do you get off calling me while I'm at home, checking me on how I handle shit?" I asked in a deathly whisper. "You thought you was gon' punk me in front of all your little flunkies, and I was just gon' let that shit slide?"

Jodeci shook his head, cracking up at my anger. "You think it's only about you making decisions? When it comes to how I handle business in these streets, I need to know that any orders I make aren't overruled. Niggas shouldn't be running behind my back to tell you to handle business, and with you supposedly being my boy, you should've deaded that shit off the bat."

"I don't have to dead a motherfucking thing. At the end of the day, when shit goes wrong I'm responsible for it. You think it's cool to push people to their breaking point? You killed two people in front of shorty and you think it ain't best to give her what she wants in trade for her silence?" I lowered my voice to a whisper. "There are two types of employees you don't want handling your product: disgruntled ones and greedy ones. Couriers come and go like nothing. I can have her and her friend replaced by the morning."

Jodeci pinched the bridge of his nose. "You think you can come up in here and throw that fast talking slick shit on me and I'm not gon' notice? Ain't no business reasons for why you let that bitch go; you let her go because you got a hard on for her."

"I don't feel shit for Nubia, but what I won't let you do is put everything I been building in jeopardy because you wanna go on a power trip." I crossed my arms and got a good look at this nigga tryna flex on me like he was about that life. I had to cool his ass down real quick before I had to put a bullet in him and his nosy ass momma. "Jodeci, we been rocking since I came here ten years ago. I know you well enough to know your current actions are way out of your regular character. What the fuck is going on?"

"I fucked up and got a bitch pregnant. This shit's got me on 100 lately," Jodeci admitted, running a hand over his dry ass waves. I knew he had to be on some other shit if he was letting go of his hair. "I'm pressing shorty to get an abortion, and she ain't with it because her parents wouldn't approve. Talking about she wasn't raised that way, yet I ain't met a hoe like her yet."

"You might have to have a couple shorties from around here have a talk with her," I said, which was code for having this gang of bitches from down the block stomp a baby out a bitch if the price is right.

Jodeci waved off the idea. "Nah, if a bitch like this get touched, the cops are coming around to ask questions. The idea of having a seed is starting to warm up on me, but it's making me hungrier for this bread."

"Jody, you already know if I'm eating then we all eating," I told him, placing a hand on his shoulder. "So long as I'm living and breathing, there will always be money for the taking."

We shared a brotherly hug and my best friend was back. He held his fist out for me to pound. "So you putting me on?"

I dapped him without hesitation. "Nigga, by the time I'm done in these streets, it's gon' be Christmas all year round. Now let's get this money."

******

After leaving Jodeci's spot, I knew there was no point in trying to return back home for rest; Estalita would have a million and one questions for where I had been, and what was going on between Jodeci and me. By no means was she about that life, and ain't have a single niche in the game except spending money, but shorty was always hanging on to every word that came out of my mouth while I was at home discussing business. For the sake of my sanity, I headed over to Niqua's house, where she whipped me up a breakfast made for a king and let me crash in her bedroom while she headed out to work as a CNA, or whatever she did that involved scrubs. I wasn't sure how long I had been out, but I woke to my phone buzzing nonstop. I had at least a hundred missed calls from everyone: Sampson, Jodeci, Vaughn, and half of them from Estalita. I got with my niggas first and found out from them what the big deal was.

"Fuck," I muttered as I checked the time on Niqua's cable box. It was six in the evening. "How the fuck did I sleep for twelve hours?"

"It's called burnout. With the way you stay in the streets it was bound to happen," Vaughn said. "Everyone is still floating in, and Sampson ain't arrive yet so you got a good hour, hour and a half tops before your absence will be noticed."

I was fully dressed and slipping into my coat when Niqua walked in holding a plate of food in her hand. Her smile dropped at the sight, and I almost felt sorry for her.

"I thought since you slept in all day you might wanna have dinner with me," she said motioning to the plate in her hand. "I made your favorite: fried chicken with wild rice and steamed broccoli."

I knew what Niqua had on that plate would be better than that nasty ass catered shit at the party, so instead of having her culinary efforts be in vain, I offered a solution. "I been sleep all day and I gotta hit the block. You wanna wrap that up for me?"

"Okay," Niqua agreed, her head bobbing up and down. "I can do that."

I accepted the glass of soda in her hand and followed her to the kitchen where she pulled out a brand new Tupperware bowl and began placing the food carefully into the container. A smile played on her lips as she prepped the food.

"So, do you have a long night ahead of you?" she asked as she sealed the container.

I accepted the food with a nonchalant shrug. "Yeah, I gotta propose to this bitch and spend the rest of my night at my engagement party."

"What?" Niqua looked stricken. Her lower lip trembled and her voice shook as she said, "You came over here and made love to me, slept in my bed, and plan on eating my food while you're on your way to get ready for forever with the next bitch? Maine, don't walk away from me like that!"

I was halfway out the front door when I peered back at her. "You knew what it was from the very beginning, Niqua. There is no love between the two of us. How can it be when a nigga ain't even been seen in public with you? Listen, I don't have time to deal with this shit right now. I'll see you this weekend."

"No, you won't! Once you walk out that door, Jermaine, don't come the fuck back!" Niqua shouted, tears streaming down her cheeks at my dissection of our FWB relationship.

I cocked my brow at her and said, "I'll see you Saturday night, Niqua. Make steak."

I checked my watch as I descended the steps. I fucked around and wasted fifteen minutes fucking around with this airhead. No matter though, I was used to working under pressure, and my presence was always worth the wait.

******

All eyes were on me when I entered the Pierre, checking out my sleek black on black Armani suit and matching loafers. While most

98

dark-skinned people liked to play off their skin tone by wearing pastels, I liked to wear muted colors that gave me the appearance of being the shadow I truly was. I glided through the crowd, dapping my niggas along the way, and approached an irate Estalita, who was surrounded by her chicas. Them bitches did nothing but down me to her on the regular, but as I approached I could see the lust in their eyes. The wanted a piece and if I determined that they could keep their mouths shut, I might break them off with a little something.

"Where have you been?" Estalita asked, crossing her arms and accepting the kiss on her cheek with mild revulsion. "Don't think you can come in here smelling good, looking good, and I'm supposed to ignore the fact that you're two hours late."

"The streets were calling," was all I said as I wrapped an arm around her waist and guided her towards the table where the Ordonez Brothers and their wives sat. I greeted the group in fluent Spanish. "Señores y señoras, buenas noches."

Estalita stared up at me in mild shock. "Have you been taking up Spanish?"

"It's part of you, so of course I'mma embrace it and learn," I lied, knowing damn well I took Spanish when I moved to America, under Sampson's orders.

That tiny piece of information made Estalita's night, and she went from being sullen to parading me around the room to all of her people. We stopped by my people and Estalita clicked with the shorty Vaughn had brought with him. She looked real familiar, and I realized she worked at the KFC. She was also at the club with Nubia. I wasn't sure whether or not she was an op, so I pulled Vaughn to the side to make sure I ain't have to worry about my business getting around.

"Nia's mad cool. Don't worry about her," Vaughn said on our walk to the bar.

"Aight," I said, glancing back and catching her and Estalita cracking up. "So, what happened with you and Drea? I thought y'all talked over the situation that happened in Miami and got back together?"

During Nubia's breakdown, Vaughn failed to hang up on the FaceTime convo he was having with Drea, which gave her a full view of the mamís I had with me. She swore up and down that Vaughn was cheating on her and basically broke up with him over some hoes he ain't see until he came out of his room. My nigga rebounded with a few shorties, and next thing I know, Drea is all over social media crying and begging for his attention. I could've sworn that Vaughn made up with her after that incident, but I guess he ain't ready to let go of the unlimited supply of pussy that comes with being single.

"Drea did what she always does: talk and not let me get a word in edgewise. That shit was cute when it was all I knew, but now that I can tell a bitch to shut the fuck and she'll do it...I'ont know if I can go back to Drea's controlling ass," Vaughn said, accepting a glass of Henny and coke from the bartender. "I mean I'm back with her, but I ain't back with her."

"So then why drag her along if you ain't feeling her?" Drea wasn't my favorite person by any means, but there was nothing worse than leading a woman on. The hurt feelings that come from a woman scorned were nothing to fuck with and could lead to a one-way trip to the grave.

Vaughn scratched the back of his neck. "It ain't as clean and simple as it looks."

"So explain it to me then."

Vaughn hesitantly opened his mouth to explain to me what was going on, but was spared by the arrival of Sampson. He wasn't alone either; on his arm was a fine ass shorty that looked equally fine as she did familiar. Once they grew closer, I recognized her as Scheherazade, Nubia's friend. I hadn't seen her since I left her and Nubia at the warehouse with a half-dead Vincent. Her eyes lit up with mutual recognition, which Sampson noticed right off the bat. The last thing I wanted was for my employer to get the wrong idea about me and shorty, so I was sure to bring up Nubia to keep the peace.

"Wassup," I said, greeting Sampson with a handshake and clap on the back. "You know in all the years I've known you, Sampson, you ain't never stepped out with someone on your arm. Wassup, Shabari. How's your girl doing?"

She rolled her eyes at the name I gave her, because I had been calling her everything under the sun since I couldn't pronounce or remember her name. "From what I can tell, she's doing good. Thanks for looking out for her when she couldn't look out for herself."

"Of course, of course," I said, smiling warmly at Estalita, who was flouncing over with Nia in tow. "I'd like to introduce the two of you to my fiancée, Estalita."

Estalita smiled as she shook hands with the couple and leaned up against me. Everything was cool until Nia laid eyes on Sampson's girl.

Her hackles rose, and I had been around enough angry females to know when a fight was getting ready to pop off, with Nia probably being the loser.

"Shahani," Nia said, looking shorty up and down. "It's good to see you landed on your feet. You always knew how to fall right into the arms of the right one."

"Maybe if you tried falling into arms and not on dicks, you could get like me too, boo," she replied, narrowing her eyes at Nia. "The only thing saving me from dragging you out of this party and giving you the ass whupping you deserve, is that you're not worth me ruining my Chanel."

Nia rolled her eyes, but I could tell her refusal to take another step near shorty meant that she knew she couldn't hold her own in a fair one. She motioned to Vaughn, who came quickly to her aide, and said, "Let's go to our seats, Daddy. I promised you that I would behave tonight, and the last thing I want is a spanking…"

"Estalita, why don't you take Shazam to get something to drink so I can catch up with Sampson?" I said, pecking her affectionately on the lips.

Estalita, who loved to gossip, answered my request and the ladies went to grab something to drink, leaving Sampson and I alone. I motioned to the bartender to bring over two tumblers of scotch on the rocks. While we waited, I figured it was time to talk business.

"I spoke with the Ordonez Brothers and they have no problem with me handling business for you until the wedding. By then, we should have someone more than capable of taking my spot."

Sampson perked his brows at the comment. "You don't think Jodeci should do it?"

"Once upon a time, my answer would've been yes without hesitation. Now, I'm not too sure. This morning, he called himself tryna make a power play on me over some hurt feelings." I accepted the tumbler of scotch set beside my shoulder. "He's got a year to get his shit together, or else I'm nominating Vaughn."

Sampson scoffed. "Vaughn? His bitch been running his life since he was in the sandbox. He ain't never set foot in the game and you think I'm gon' let him be in charge of my shit? Nah…"

"Sampson, trust me; he might not show it, but Vaughn can be ruthless when he wants to be. Don't even worry about none of this. I got you regardless," I promised, sipping my drink.

"Well don't forget that you got some loose ends to tie up before our business relationship is finished entirely. You are one of my most solid hittas, and I don't know where that bitch is and what nigga she might have plotting to come after me when she finds out the truth." Sampson mimicked my actions as he surveyed the party. "I need you to handle her by the time you walk down that aisle and say 'I do.'"

"You already know that ain't nothing but a thing," I said with a sigh. "You at least got the girl's name?"

"Apollo moved them out of town long before Donna gave birth, so I never found out what her name was, but I'm sure you can put your ear to the streets and figure something out." Sampson clapped me on the back. "Enough about that, though. Get up there and make it official with your girl."

I sauntered up to the stage and did just that. There were hoots and hollers from the crowd as I motioned for Estalita join me. For someone that planned this entire party and picked out her ring, Estalita played surprised pretty well, even tearing up when I pulled the Tiffany's box out of my pocket and got down on one knee. She didn't even make me work for it, exclaiming, "yes" before I even got to "marry." When I placed the four-carat engagement ring on her finger, I paused for a split second, thinking of how I could've seen myself placing this ring on the hand of another woman. The only one to ever make this thug feel something. It was too late for all of that now. I chose the streets because if I knew anything about love, it was that it was likely to let me down.

Shahani

I held my glass of champagne tight in my hand as I watched Maine propose to his Mexican Barbie. She was beautiful—with one of the best bodies that money could buy—and I didn't doubt for a second that her father spared no expense. I noticed that she spoke perfect English and was smart, albeit a little spoiled. The bottom line was, as much as I wanted to hate on her, I couldn't because she was nice. She was also madly in love with Maine and from the looks of it, he was feeling her, too. Nubia fucked up when she let him walk away, and I couldn't even tell her so because everything that came out of my mouth towards her was seen as poison, with good reason. I was still replaying the night on the ride home.

Sampson must've taken my silence as anger because he pulled me close and kissed me on the forehead, "I hope you ain't pouting over that party back there. That wasn't nothing but a business deal. Everything that glitters ain't gold."

"What is that supposed to mean?"

"It means that sometimes you gotta sacrifice the small things for the bigger picture. He ain't suffering, though; it's plenty of niggas wishing they had the balls he did to make that shit happen," Sampson replied in an offhand manner. "Now what else has you upset? Your cousin talking shit?"

I tried shoving the animosity I had to Nia deep down so I could enjoy my night, but I couldn't shake what she said to me in front of everyone. Was I really a hustler hopper? Yes, my last three boyfriends have saved me from unfortunate circumstances, but is that a bad thing? I wasn't going to mention it to Sampson, but he did ask.

"Do you think there's something wrong with me always ending up being saved by a man? I mean, it's not like I got with you or any of my exes because of what they could do for me. I loved Lonzo, I loved Donovan, and…I love you, too. You don't have to say it back or anything but—"

Sampson tilted my head up and placed a gentle kiss on my lips. "I love you, Shahani. I planned on telling you somewhere more romantic, like over dinner after seeing a nice show, but the moment doesn't matter: you do. Don't let the hateful words of a simple bitch like that get in the way of how we feel for each other."

"I won't," I promised, instantly soothed by his words.

We sat in a companionable silence, with me resting my head on Sampson's lap as he ran his fingers through my hair. I was half asleep when the car stopped in the middle of an unknown neighborhood. My first instinct was that something was wrong, but one look at Sampson's face told me that I didn't have anything to worry about. He helped me out of the car and into an empty storefront. The lights came on and I spun around, taking in the large floor space that could easily fit ten salon chairs comfortably. The floors were polished solid oak and the walls were sparkling white. All this place needed was the right fixtures and furniture.

"You like it?" Sampson asked, wrapping his arms around my waist. "This was supposed to be your birthday present, but I couldn't help myself. I hate seeing you look sad and I had to make you smile again."

"This is…this is mine?" I squeaked. "You got this place for me?"

"I came across your journal with the swatches and pictures you had for your dream salon. I could see you were growing a little bored being cooped up in the house all day long with nothing to do since you got fired from your job over that nonsense." He squeezed me tight and nestled into my neck. "We're a team, Shahani, and I want to see you grow and watch your dreams come true. You can decorate this place however you want, money ain't a problem."

I leaned into his embrace, smiling as the dreams that I worked tireless nights for came true when I least expected it. "What did I do to deserve you?"

"You haven't done anything but be true to me," Sampson replied. "That's all I ever need from you."

That was nothing for a girl like me. It was nothing to reply, "You got it."

******

Sampson's gift of my dream shop gave me a new purpose. I went from being bored in the house all day to out and about shopping for furniture, equipment, and advertising materials. Sampson stayed true to his word too; I woke up to an Amex Experian card with my name on it and a note saying, *have fun*. I most certainly was with the way I was swiping. The past three weeks were a blur, and I forgot all about

Nia and her hateful ass comments until Pinky walked into the salon as I was conducting interviews. I did a double take at the sight; I knew she just got finished working her shift judging by her attire. Her sudden appearance had me so thrown that I could barely pay attention to the girl I was interviewing. Her portfolio was dope and her resume impeccable. I hired her on the spot and closed up shop so I could pay attention to Pinky, who was sitting in a corner on a leather stool, willing herself invisible.

I locked the front door and flipped the sign to *Out to Lunch*. Taking a seat next to her on my white leather sofa, I asked, "Pinky, what are you doing here? Donovan will have a fit if he catches you anywhere near me."

"I know, but I knew I had to come here and try anyway," Pinky said, running a hand over her tousled wig. "Shahani, I need you...the girls need you, too. Donovan's out of control, and it's only a matter of time that one of us ends up dead. You know Tasty is in jail because he didn't pay her bail? He beat Candy within an inch of her life because she was short $10. As it turned out, the money was stuck together and she had it all along."

I placed a hand on my chest at the news; I had always been stern with them, but those girls were like misguided little sisters to me. I know Donovan can be abusive—I've felt his wrath a time or two—but I never thought it would get to the point that he became one of those pimps, the kind that rules with a fist instead of reason. It broke my heart to hear things were going bad for the girls and broke it even deeper to know there was nothing I could do about it.

"Pinky…"

"Shahani, please don't say what I think you're about to say—"

"There isn't much I can do. I'm out of the life and I don't plan on going back. Plus, I promised my new boyfriend that I would stay away from Donovan, which is easy to do after he played me for my cousin."

Pinky pounded her hand as she spoke. "Who do you think is the reason for all of this bad shit happening, Shahani? Nia's got it in her head that she's running shit, and Donovan allows it. Some of the girls aren't getting paid and when we ask, she tells Donovan we're questioning his authority." She reached out for my hand and squeezed it. "Please, Shahani, do something for us."

I mulled over my options and said, "I can possibly get the girls a part-time job at another KFC where I'm cool with the manager, and one of my homegirls is a manager at Burger King. I'm also looking for a few shampoo girls. The pay is minimum wage, but you'll be able to take home everything in your pocket."

"Shahani, trapping is all I know. I dropped out of high school when I was fourteen and I've been on my own since then. I don't have any skills, and how far is being a shampoo girl gonna get me? I need to use my body while it's still worth using."

I placed my other hand over hers and gave it a gentle squeeze. "Pinky, it might not be the perfect job, but it's a stepping stone to get you somewhere. I'm not saying that there aren't success stories, but most girls in the life end up in jail or dead. Is that where you wanna be?"

"No," Pinky said, wiping a tear from her eye.

"Take this job as shampoo girl, and let's get you started on the path to something better."

"What about my bills? I can't wait around to start work because my landlord—"

"Don't worry about that. I'll put something together for you and whatever girls wanna leave Donovan behind," I said, thinking I could maybe renovate the space above the shop and make it an apartment.

Pinky's tears fell harder, and she couldn't hold them back any longer. I pulled her in for a hug, rubbing her back and being the comfort she desperately needed. I knew what it was like to have your back against the wall and no solution in sight. That was my life when I was younger, and I've been fighting to make sure I never get that low again. Pinky left on a mission to recruit whatever girls were interested, while I went back to setting up the receptionist's station in between interviews. Three girls later I had a new visitor, one I wanted nothing to do with. Unlike with Pinky, I drew this interview out as long as I could in the hopes that another girl would come and Donovan couldn't try anything. I had no such luck and decided to deal with this monster sooner rather than later.

"You need to leave," I told Donovan as I stood next to one of my fully stocked stations. It was nothing to grab a pair of shears and get to work on his ass if need be. "We said everything we needed to say when I caught you in bed fucking my cousin."

"You still mad about that? Baby, I was breaking her in," Donovan said, taking a tentative step forward which propelled me two steps back. "You're the only woman I'll ever love, Shahani, and I want you to come home."

I crossed my arms and shook my head at the audacity of this nigga. "You think you can come in here with some simp ass apology and expect me to come home to you? Home, where you fucked the shit out my cousin? Home, where my job was to build you up and put my dreams on hold? Home, where you used to put your hands on me?"

"I only put my hands on you when you got out of line," Donovan defended.

"You shouldn't have put them on me at all if you truly loved me," I shot back, my throat growing tight. "I'm happy with Sampson. Look at this; he believes in me enough to invest in my dream. He cares about my feelings and I don't feel inferior to him. This is the life I've been dreaming of. This is the life I deserve."

"What about the life our girls deserve? You just up and left them with no goodbye or nothing."

I scoffed. "The girls know where to find me. They also know if they need anything, like to get away from you and your bullshit, they can call me and I got them. I don't need your permission or approval to be in their life."

"What if I gave you a store of your own?" Donovan said, holding his hands out. "I got the bread stacked. I can put fifty stacks in your hand and you can make this shit happen, Shahani. If money is what you want and need to come home, then I'll give you money. But I need you back."

"And I needed a real man and it took mine selling me for me to find one. You are your own worst enemy, Donovan," I said, pointing at him. "It took for you to see me happy and building with someone, for you to come and offer me what you know I've been dreaming about for the longest? I'm cool on that. Give that $50,000 to Nia and let her make all your dreams come true, because I'm over and done with you."

Since begging, pleading, and trying to appease me didn't work, Donovan went to the next best thing: scare tactics. The pained mask he wore dropped, and I could see his true façade, one of pure evil. This nigga changed moods like he changed clothes, and I had been too stuck in being with him to realize it until now.

"So that's how you feel?" Donovan asked, reaching in his pocket and pulling out a switchblade. He flicked it open and punctured my leather sofa, slicing a long, irreparable line across it. "Aight, Shahani, I'll play this game with you. You feeling yourself, your shit ain't stinking yet 'cause this nigga got you feeling untouchable. That'll come to an end real soon though, and I'll be back to claim what belongs to me. Have fun, Shahani, because when I come back for you, I'm putting you to work."

Donovan waved and left as quietly as he came. I hadn't realized it, but I was shaking from head to toe. He may have been arrogant, abusive, bitter, and angry, but there was one thing that Donovan has been since day one: a man of his word. He was coming back, and I had to be ready to fight for my life at a moment's notice. If he wanted to bring the heat then I would bring the burn.

Nubia

Marlee jumped up and down as she held the princess dress in her hand. "Can I have this one for my birthday, Nubia? Please?"

I checked the price tag of the Deluxe Princess Belle costume and sighed inwardly. At $89.95, this dress was sixty dollars out of my price range. I wanted to tell Marlee that maybe I could get her the same dress at Target or even a cute Belle shirt for $15.95, but that would break her spirit more than it had been since she discovered that her mother wasn't coming home. Of course I didn't tell her Precious had been murdered, but children were perceptive as fuck, and little Marlee spoke as if she would miss her mother with a sense of finality that revealed she knew she was gone. I had been keeping her spirits lifted by adding the finishing touches to the birthday party Precious had planned to a tee.

"Of course you can have this dress," I said, placing it into the mesh basket and tugging her to the accessories wall. "You can't have a dress without your shoes and tiara, now can you?"

We spent a good chunk of time laughing and playing with tiaras, wands in front of the magic mirror with the help of a cast member. Marlee was smiling one of her first genuine smiles since this entire ordeal, and I felt my heart melt. When my parents were killed I was placed straight into foster care. There was no laughing and smiling;

just a cold cot and being ushered from one cold home to the next. I couldn't have little Marlee struggling the way I did. She would be happy even if it meant I had to spread a bill or two out.

"Nubia," Marlee asked as we made our way to the maternity section of the store, "do you think my dad will come like he promised to?"

Ever since Precious was killed, I had been searching high and low for Marlee's father, Sullivan. Most of Precious' family had cut ties with her and didn't even want to help me keep custody of Marlee, let alone give me a general direction of where her father might be. All I had so far was his name, and it hadn't gotten me anywhere. I didn't have the heart to tell Marlee because it would be like telling her she had become an orphan by default.

"I'm sure he'll come to celebrate your fifth birthday with you," I replied. To take her attention off of pressing matters at hand, I pointed to a cute little three piece set and asked, "Do you think the baby would like that outfit?"

Marlee loved picking out baby outfits, and was instantly distracted by the task of finding something cute for my daughter to wear home from the hospital. I touched my belly, soaking in the feel of her fluttering kicks. My belly seemed to have ballooned overnight; one minute I was making due with jeans and sweaters and the next I had to give up denim for leggings and tunics. Although she wasn't created from the best circumstances, I loved my baby girl with all my heart.

I was rubbing my belly and smiling at Marlee when I got the feeling that I was being watched. My eyes searched the section and locked with my aunt's. She looked down at my belly and back at me, her expression cold. My cousin, Ashanti, appeared and although it was small, I could see her pregnancy bump through the sundress she was wearing.

Ashanti's brows furrowed in concern at her mother's sudden change in attitude. "Ma, what's—oh my God. Come on, ma. You don't need any of that negativity in your life."

"No," Vivica choked out, gently shrugging out of Ashanti's grip as she tried to lead her out of the store. "We came here to get something for my granddaughter, and that's what we'll do."

Marlee came running up to me with a beautiful little onesie. "Rhea should wear this home. I think she'll look really pretty in it."

"So do I," I said, placing the pajama into my shopping basket with a trembling hand. "Now how about we check out and grab something to eat, okay?"

We had barely cleared the baby section when Vivica called out to me. My body obliged her before my mind did; my mind was still running away from her hateful glare while my body stopped and turned halfway to oblige her. She took slow, calculated steps towards me, with Ashanti following behind, her expression unsure. I braced myself for an attack, but I knew a distinguished woman like Vivica would never put her hands on me in public for fear that she would ruin her image. When she got within an arm's length she reached out and touched my stomach.

"This is your baby with your husband?" she asked, rubbing my belly softly.

I nodded my head slowly. "Yeah."

"You're having a girl, huh." I nodded again. "Well, I hope that for everything you've done to my marriage, your child suffers for it. I also hope your marriage is filled with the misery mine had been drenched in since you came along."

I backed up and pushed her hand off of my stomach. "You don't have to do that. My marriage is ruined because I spent so much time trying to get out of your hellhole of a house and away from your monster of a husband, I went right into the arms of another. And I'm sure that whatever you tried to curse my child with is the reason why you can't have any of your own."

Vivica slipped up and slapped me, the sound reverberating throughout the store. Onlookers gasped and Marlee started crying. Ashanti, catching her perfect mother acting out of character, grabbed Vivica and pulled her out of the store. Cast members rushed to my aide, asking me if they wanted to have Vivica detained by security while they called the police. I politely thanked them for their concern, but Vivica had done something I never imagined she would in a million years. She proved to the world that I wasn't crazy, and she was the monster she never claimed to be.

******

It was hard to get Marlee to forget about the incident at the Disney Store, but I finally succeeded when I bought her a Happy Meal for dinner and ice cream for dessert. I was laying it on thick by spoiling her this much, but I couldn't help it; she was such a sweet little girl and how could I say no? I couldn't, that's how. Once she was tucked in, I headed to my bedroom and began stuffing the goody bags for the birthday party tomorrow morning. I had found everything I needed in Precious' closet, including the receipts for the cake and payment for the American Girl party, which made it a little easier to get through all of this. I was placing the finishing touches on the bag when I heard the front door open followed by the chattering of Precious' aunt, Myrna. Once I showed up with Marlee at the precinct to report Precious missing, the cops made note of how they would have to place her in temporary foster care until her family was found. The only person that answered any of my calls was Myrna, and in trade for her helping me keep Marlee, I let her take Precious' bedroom rent-free.

"Hello, Miss Thing," Myrna said as she sashayed through the house with her boyfriend, Bernard, in tow, both of them looking high as fuck. "I wasn't expecting you to be up at this time. Usually you're knocked out on the couch."

"Well Marlee's birthday party is tomorrow so I have to make sure everything is perfect. Is everyone still coming?"

Myrna didn't answer off the bat; instead she made a face and disappeared into the kitchen with her male friend tagging behind her. She emerged with two bottles of Budweiser and said, "I spoke to Precious' cousins and they said they would come. My sister on the other hand, I don't think she's coming. That beef she has with Precious runs deep and they still have some unresolved issues."

"But Precious isn't going to be there," I said, my tone laced with exasperation.

"We don't know that. Last I checked Precious is just missing.

Ain't that what you told the police?" Myrna said with a hint of malice. "Unless there's something you ain't telling me?"

I placed my head into my hands and shook my head back and forth for a minute. "No, Myrna. You're right; Precious might show up. But don't you think her mother might want to take this chance to talk with her daughter if she does show up?"

"Precious has been running away since she was fifteen-years-old. If there's one day she wouldn't miss for the world, it's Marlee's birthday. For that reason, my sister would rather stay away because she's tired of the drama. She said she might send a gift though."

"Have you at least gotten a lead on Marlee's father?"

Myrna shrugged once again. "I put feelers out to a few friends, but I haven't heard anything back."

"Okay," I said, running my hands through my hair. "I guess I'll see you in the morning then. You're still coming to help bring the cake, right?"

"Of course I will. Now get off your feet and let that baby get some rest," Myrna said, shooing me to my room.

I did as I was told, only because I did need to get off my feet and rest; Marlee and I had been out since early in the morning. I had an appointment at WIC followed by a checkup at the doctor's office. Once we finished with appointments, we spent the rest of the day in the city looking around and trying to find me a nice, cheap outfit to wear at the party. I settled with a cheap maxi dress from Forever 21 and some of those cheap fur slides. I was guaranteed to be on the move all day tomorrow and wanted to be comfortable. I was still up tossing and turning over everything I had planned when I thought I heard Marlee's room door open. I only knew it was hers because it stuck whenever it opened or closed. I listened for a moment, waiting to hear her pad to the bathroom or come knocking on my bedroom door like she did whenever she got scared, but after five minutes neither sound came.

I opened my bedroom door quietly and looked around before heading down the hall to Marlee's room, passing the bathroom on my way. The door was wide open, which had my hair standing up on the back of my neck. I immediately went back to the kitchen and grabbed a frying pan and knife from the dish rack. Myrna had her faults, with the biggest one being that she got high, but over the past three weeks she had been nothing but kind to Marlee. I would hope in my heart that she wouldn't bring a man in here and leave him unsupervised. My worse fears were confirmed when I quietly opened Marlee's room door and saw that she wasn't alone. Bernard was sitting at the edge of Marlee's bed whispering to her. I heard her whimper and knew something was wrong. I didn't ask any questions, I just ran up on him, swinging the frying pan and hitting him square in the back. The blow was enough to send him toppling to the floor in shock.

"What the fuck!" he shouted, looking up at me like I was crazy. "What the fuck is wrong with you?"

"What are you doing in here with her?!" I screamed.

The lights turned on and I saw Marlee sitting in bed crying, unharmed. Myrna came rushing to the aid of her boyfriend, helping him to his feet. My chest was heaving from adrenaline, and I wasn't dropping my knife until I knew Marlee was fine.

"Marlee, are you okay?" I asked calmly as I kept my eyes on the couple in front of me. "What happened, sweetheart?"

"I miss my mommy," Marlee cried, plopping back into her pillow and howling.

Bernard held his hands up, begging me with his eyes to put the knife and frying pan down. "I was on my way to the kitchen to get something to drink when I heard her crying. All I was trying to do was make sure she was okay. Precious was like a daughter to me, and I would never do her daughter like that."

"Me and Bernard might have our ways, but we ain't down with none of that fucked up shit," Myrna said, her tone cold. "My mother sold me when I was Marlee's age to grown men for a hit. I started smoking to escape that shit. Who was it for you?"

I dropped my weapons. "My aunt."

Myrna and Bernard held their hands out for my weapons, which I handed them with no argument. I took Marlee into my bedroom with me, where I swore to have her sleep until I could give her to her father. We both cried that night, with me comforting her for the loss of her mother as I cried for the innocence I lost, and the misplaced hate in my heart I replaced it with.

******

Despite a night of crying, Marlee was all smiles at her birthday party. American Girl was filled with her classmates and little cousins. I sat on the sidelines talking with Cheyenne, one of Precious' cousins. They were tight, and it pained me to have to lie to her face as she spoke about Precious with such affection. Apparently Marlee wasn't the only one who was convinced that Precious wasn't returning; they all spoke of her in past tense, and I finally found out why.

"You didn't hear this from me, but word on the block is that Paco fucked around and got my cousin killed," Cheyenne said as she sipped on her Voss water. "One of his boys from the south is a Facebook friend of mine, and he mentioned that Precious, Marlee, and Paco were supposed to come down there with some product so they could start over. I'm guessing shit went wrong, Precious got caught up, and them niggas murked her."

That was exactly what happened. "You think the cops have gotten anywhere with the investigation?"

"Probably not; whoever she was working for was real thorough. I wouldn't be surprised if they had some people on payroll making sure Precious' file went missing. She'll be another forgotten black girl in the system." Cheyenne reached out and patted my belly. "You know, Nubia, you're a real godsend right now. Not everyone would stay and take care of someone else's child. I would've taken in Marlee but my prior ACS case makes it impossible. Honestly, I think she's better off with you than any of our family. If there's anything you need for her, lemme know and I got you."

"If you could point me in the direction of anyone willing to hire a pregnant woman that would be great," I said, rubbing my belly for effect. "I've been looking and no one will touch me, not even for seasonal. I have enough cash stacked to get us through the summer, but that's it."

"What about welfare or food stamps?"

I sighed. "My husband makes too much."

"Husband?"

"Girl, it's a long story. Long, and tragic as hell. But that nigga doesn't plan on being here for me or our child, and despite that, I know he won't divorce me because that would mean paying alimony and child support."

Cheyenne took a long sip of her water and shook her head. "Girl, you better than me, because I would've been went *Waiting to Exhale* on his ass. If you put a ring on my finger and a baby in my womb, you're gonna run me my money or see me until you're sick of me. Just like that."

I wish I would roll up on Vincent demanding money. He would probably beat the baby out of me. We had been doing such a good job of staying out of each other's lives, and I wanted to keep it that way. I would make a way without his help, even if that meant standing on the corner passing out flyers. Those were the only quick jobs that came to mind, except Cheyenne had something a little more real in mind.

"I can't promise you anything great right now, but when you drop that baby, I can guarantee you a spot on the pole at my job, the Pole Palace. The tips are amazing and if the right baller walks through the door, you can easily cash out."

"You want me to strip?" I said, placing my hand on my chest. "Don't get me wrong, I have nothing against strippers at all, but I don't have enough rhythm to be on a pole."

Cheyenne cracked up at my innocence. "Girl, no stripper just gets up there and knows what they're doing. You get onstage remembering that you've got mouths to feed, rent to pay, knowing it's this or selling your pussy, and you make something happen. If you're that scared, I can help you out once you drop your load. That is, if you're down."

I wasn't sure if I would ever be down with getting on a pole to make money. Part of me feared that it would make me more desirable than I had become. Shahani had stripped before we met, but her beauty was bound to get her chose and off a pole. Me, on the other hand, I knew in my heart of hearts that Vincent was the best I could do. My best option was finding myself a nice guy that would be able to overlook my shortcomings and take me as I am. I knew he wouldn't do that knowing other men had viewed my body.

Cheyenne sensed my hesitance and said, "Boo, you got two options: a pole or your husband. Which one are you choosing?"

******

Marlee's brows furrowed at the sight of Slick Cutz. The usual niggas were posted in front of the Brooklyn location, shooting the shit and looking at anything that walked by in a skirt. Whatever eyes weren't on me locked on Marlee, who was still wearing her Belle costume. Her American Girl doll was clutched tightly in her hand as she surveyed her new surroundings. I was just as scared to be here myself, especially since I hadn't seen Vincent since I dropped him off at the hospital. I prayed that being in a public place would keep him from doing anything stupid, like trying to hurt me.

"Vincent," I said, approaching his chair slowly.

He paused mid cut, cutting off his clippers and turning around. I swallowed at the sight: his jaw was still swollen from being broken, the swelling from his eyes had just cleared up, and I could see that his nose was slightly crooked. Maine had done damage to Vincent, and I knew I would be the one to pay for it. I backed up slowly, thinking I had to be crazy to think it was okay to show up at this nigga's job for money, knowing I was the reason why he had lost out on so much.

"No, don't run away," he said, sounding like he had a wad of tissue in his mouth. "What you came here for?"

"I…I…I wanted to talk to you about our child. In private," I said, looking around the shop, shrinking at all the eyes on me. "It'll only be a minute."

Vincent shook his head. "If you think I would go anywhere alone with you, you must be out of your fucking mind. Speak your peace here or get the fuck outta my shop."

"I need money. It doesn't have to be a lot, but something, anything would help. I need to start looking for a cheap stroller, crib, a carrier since they won't let me take her out the hospital without one…" I stopped talking as Vincent began to laugh. "Vincent—"

Vincent held up a hand, cutting me off instantly. "You think after letting that nigga snatch me out of my shop and damn near kill me that I owe you a motherfucking thing?"

"I saved you from him—"

"You saved me because that's what the fuck you were supposed to do," Vincent spat, causing me to recoil. "I take you out of your aunt's house, make you my wife, and you repay me by putting some other nigga in our business? I don't owe you shit."

I held my stomach. "You put this baby in me, the least you could do is care about her."

"I hope the little bitch dies," Vincent said without mercy. "And I hope you join her, you stupid, ungrateful bitch. I'm not giving you a fucking thing except a divorce when I fucking feel like it."

Marlee clutched my hand. "Nubia, can we go?"

"Yeah, Marlee," I choked out, turning away from Vincent so he wouldn't see me cry. "Let's go home."

"Yeah, take that nigga Sullivan's kid back to him, and tell him to stay the fuck outta my shop." I stopped walking. "Oh, you thought I wouldn't know you showed up here with another nigga's kid? I been looking at his ass every Tuesday for the past year. You probably met him here, huh? Looking at niggas on the low like you was doing with Maine?"

I exited out of the shop with my head hung, avoiding the piercing looks that came at me from every direction, some shaking their heads while others simply stared in disgust. Wiping my eyes, I decided it was time to make a decision on how I would proceed now that I knew where I stood with Vincent. As if on cue, I felt a flutter in my stomach. In a matter of months I would have another mouth to feed. My time of having people look out for me and take care of me was gone, and now I had to look out for myself and mine. It was time to hustle and make some real money, which was why I called Cheyenne with a heavy heart.

"Why am I not surprised to hear from you," she said with a laugh. "Remember: from this day on, you can't trust none of these niggas to do for you. Get this money for yourself and by your damn self. You understand?"

"Yeah," I said without hesitation. "Let's get this money."

Maine

Six months later...

*E*stalita sunk into her seat, scoffing and rolling her eyes for a third time in the past fifteen minutes. She had been in a fucked up mood all day, and I wasn't about to sit here and play Dr. Phil with her ass. It was bad enough that I didn't feel like showing up to this baby shower; I wasn't in the mood to deal with one of her temper tantrums. She was likely to fuck with me and end up on the side of the road. Or at least that's where I would consider leaving her before picking her back up. Them bitches she called friends might as well be informants because every little thing that happened in our relationship made its way right back to Salvador. Our first argument over setting a date for the wedding ended with Salvador reminding me that he had given me two special gifts of his and how I needed to take care of them. I would take care of this bitch alright—

"I just don't understand why we have to go when you're not even friends with Jodeci anymore," Estalita huffed, crossing her arms and legs as she angrily glared straight ahead.

"Since when am I not friends with Jodeci?"

"Because he didn't show up to our engagement party until it was over. What kind of friend does that? Plus, I haven't heard you say a word about him," Estalita said with a shrug.

"He showed up late because he had business to handle, and the reason why you don't hear about him is because I don't discuss work at home. That's still my brother though," I said, and it was partially true.

Ever since the blowup at Jodeci's house, we patched everything up, but I still felt like he had some shit on his chest that he wasn't addressing. If he thought I would kiss his ass to find out what was wrong then he was fucking with the wrong one. I came to this country with nothing but the clothes on my back and vague memories of the family I once had; if I couldn't cry over my blood, then what would make them think I would cry over a bond? No one had a permanent place in my heart because I had very little expectations of people to begin with.

Including my irritating fiancée.

"How long are we staying?" Estalita whined as we pulled up to the party hall. "Can I just wait in the car?"

"How about on the day of our wedding I stay home and let you say 'I do' to all them bitches you be with?" I countered. "Hmmm? If I can sit through parties and dinners with your people, then you can do the same for mine, and if you can't, then maybe you need to find a new way out of your pop's house."

That shut her right the fuck up.

I felt my waist for my burner, checked my line up in the rearview mirror, and made sure there wasn't a stray thread out of place on my Yves Saint Laurent tee. Estalita preened herself as well, doing a hair toss and smoothing the front of the blush sweater dress she wore. I stepped around the car and helped her out like a gentleman, which caused a small commotion. That, and my black Maserati Quattroporte. It was a gift to myself for moving the most weight out of the entire organization over the past five months. I didn't enter this game as a dope boy, but part of being a successful hitta was studying people. I had studied long and hard enough to know what moves to make, and it benefitted me in the long run. I was building my kingdom swiftly and knew exactly how to protect it.

"Damn, Maine."

"My nigga pulled out the Maserati?"

"Yo, I ain't never seen shorty before. My nigga, Maine, fucked around and got a foreign."

Niggas were ogling my car and my bitch, plotting in vain on how they could get like me. I dapped them and kept it pushing, not in the mood for small talk or pretending I gave a fuck about them when they knew I didn't. The party hall was lavishly decorated, with Jodeci and his baby moms sitting on the throne. I couldn't front; shorty was bad and bougie. I could tell by the way she surveyed the room: like everyone was beneath her, she was bored by their presence, and if she had her way, she wouldn't even be in attendance. This type of attitude threw me; Jodeci usually went for goofy broads that liked to laugh. Just by getting a look at shorty and the tight faced woman next to her that had to be her moms, I really wanted to hear the story behind how they met.

"Bro, you made it," Jodeci said, hopping out of his chair and pulling me in for a brotherly hug. He hugged Estalita as well, greeting her with a warm, "Wassup, Estalita."

"Hola, Jodeci," Estalita simpered like she wasn't just pitching a fit only minutes ago. "*Felicidades por el bebe.*"

"*Gracias, gracias,*" Jodeci replied as he sat back in his seat. "I'd like you to meet my baby moms"—shorty cleared her throat—"the mother of my child, Ashanti, and her mother, Vivica. Ashanti, Vivica, this is my brother, Maine, and his fiancée, Estalita."

Ashanti, impressed by the Jacob & Co. watch on my wrist and Estalita's engagement ring sparkling underneath the dim lighting, decided that we were worthy of a warm greeting. "Nice to meet the both of you. Jodeci has said nothing but kind words about you, Maine. Are those this season's Dolce and Gabbana pumps?"

Estalita did a little jig and replied, "*Sí,* I have a girl that allows me to shop the presale."

At the mention of designer clothing and shoes, both women clicked, giving me time to catch up with my boy. Or at least I thought I would, until Vivica followed us out back where partygoers were chilling and firing up blunts. I could pretend like I ain't know what ma'dukes was up to, but after dealing with Jodeci's thirsty ass momma, I knew what this was about.

"Jodeci, dear, can you bring me a glass of red wine please? I'll be sure to keep your friend company while you're gone," Vivica said, reaching into the pocket of her pantsuit and pulling out a cigarette. She perched it between her lips, and purred, "You got a light?"

I pulled out my lighter, watching as she sucked in her cheeks and closed her eyes like she was giving top. Her eyes fluttered open as she let out a steady stream of smoke to the side. All I could think to myself was, *where the fuck is Jodeci with the drinks?* "So, Maine, you've known Jodeci for almost half of your life: do you think he's ready for fatherhood? Does he have what it takes to be a provider?"

"Hell yeah," I said, and meant it too. "I was a child soldier in Sierra Leone. When they rescued me from the war I got counseling and shit, but it wasn't enough to fully fix the damage that had been done to me. When I got here, my boy looked out for me and made sure that I was good. Honestly, I don't think I would've assimilated as well as I did if it wasn't for Jodeci keeping everyone from picking on the awkward African kid. We've known each other for the past ten years, and if there was one person I know that's capable of doing what he has to for his new family, it's Jodeci."

Vivica mulled over my words, ingesting them right along with her cigarette. When she was finished, she countered with, "So if you feel this way, then why won't you put in a word for him?"

The question caught me off guard, and I felt like I was being ambushed. "Excuse me?"

"You heard me: you believe in him enough to be your friend, but he isn't good enough to take over?"

"How the fuck did this go from making sure your daughter is good to checking me on how I run shit?" I took a step towards her and said in a voice barely above a whisper, "I don't know what Jodeci told you about me, but he must've failed to mention that although I may be a hustler in America, I'll always have a soldier's heart. Fuck with me if you want to, and I'll make sure you meet your grandchild before everyone else does."

I swear this bitch just creamed her panties. Vivica tried to play scared, but I could see it in her eyes that had we been anywhere but a backyard full of people, she would've been begging a nigga to choke her. She collected herself and said politely, "My intentions weren't to intrude on how you run your business—"

"Then don't," I cut her off. She got to biting and sucking on her lower lip on some real freak shit, which prompted me to begin looking for her son-in-law. "Where the fuck is Jodeci at anyway?"

As if on cue, Jodeci reappeared holding two bottles of beer and a glass of red wine. Vivica accepted the glass with a smile and raised her glass to me. She glanced over my shoulder and her entire demeanor changed. I didn't even have to turn around to know her husband showed up. Jodeci's friendly wave solidified it. The smile he wore slipped from his face when he caught sight of mine.

"Oh, there's my Cornell," Vivica simpered, like she wasn't just openly hitting on me seconds ago. "I'll leave you boys to it…"

I waited for her to float across the room to her husband, a well-dressed man in his late forties, before I got into Jodeci's ass about this.

"So you speaking on how I handle business to outsiders now?" I asked, taking a swig of my beer and watching him play confused. "Why the fuck was your mother-in-law over here telling me about how I need to promote you? What, that bitch tryna make you the best drug dealer you can be?"

Jodeci's expression was apologetic. "She spoke to you? Fuck man…Maine, you know I would never—"

"Never what? Have conversations about me and the way I run shit behind my back? This ain't a fucking game. This decision isn't one that I make based off of what I'm feeling at the moment. I'm looking for you to prove that you deserve it—"

"Oh, because you deserved it?" Jodeci scoffed. "Don't forget that we been down riding since day one, nigga. I've had your back when you wasn't no-fucking-body and the least you could do is have mine when I need it. I would never make you jump through hoops for a fucking promotion."

"Making you give me complete confidence in you is some hoops?"

"It is, considering that you only got where you are by fucking the connect's daughter," Jodeci hissed. "Salvador was so concerned with making sure that his daughter was good, that he gave you the keys to the kingdom, and you're telling me you can't look out for me in the same way? Nigga, I made you."

"You made me?" I asked, pointing to my chest in mild disbelief.

Jodeci looked at me up and down. "You wouldn't be half the man you are without my help."

"I'm willing to recognize you for helping me assimilate into American culture, but Jodeci: you ain't make me. Being snatched from my mother's arms and drafted into war is what made me. Watching women be raped then butchered right in front of my eyes made me. Killing like I was a fucking machine is what made me. I've always been this ruthless motherfucker; all you did was put a bow on him."

"That's how the fuck you feel?" Jodeci said, taking a step towards me.

I closed the space between us. "I thought I made it clear that I don't have those."

Everyone in the backyard had stopped what they were doing to watch the scene. I wasn't crazy enough to start no shit in the middle of a baby shower with all these people present. Whatever business I had to settle with Jodeci would be dealt with on the streets, and I hoped for his sake that he popped first because when I take aim, I don't plan on missing.

******

"That nigga said what?" Vaughn asked, staring at me wide-eyed as he took another shot of Patrón. "Nah, I don't wanna believe my mans would say something like that…"

I glanced over at Vaughn, who was getting a lap dance from a thick ass red bone, and nodded my head slowly. "Believe it, nigga. I had to remind him that he may have helped me fit in, but he ain't shape me into who I am today. That bitch and her moms must've been amping him up, 'cause I ain't never known Jodeci to say or think some outlandish shit like that."

"You know how these niggas get. They find a new piece of pussy and start changing." Vaughn caught the look I gave him and said, "What?"

"I know you not over here talking about changing over some pussy when you been juggling Drea and Nia for the past five months."

Vaughn slid another single between the stripper's G-string and gave her a slap on the ass. "I already told you; that's a completely different situation. I'm in a relationship with Drea and Nia is nothing more than a friend."

"A friend you always rushing off to see in the middle of the night," I noted as I scanned the strip club. "You ain't gotta lie to me."

"I ain't lying; it's just a complicated situation. How about this? Instead of focusing on what I got going on and whatever shiesty shit Jodeci might be plotting, you need to take a look around this club and find something to take home for the night. Start with a dance on me."

I shot him a *nigga really* look. "I own the club. I can have any bitch in here that I damn well please. Especially the new ones. They stay throwing it at a nigga on the regular. Speaking of regular..."

One of my girls, Cheyenne, was at the bar talking to the bartender, and motioned to the general direction of the VIP section where Vaughn and I sat. They wrapped the convo up when she was given a platter with a bottle of Ace of Spades and four flutes of champagne. I watched as she slinked over to us, swaying her denim clad hips with every step she took as her breasts jiggled, straining to be free of the rhinestone bikini top she wore. Vaughn's stripper finished up, and he sent her on her way as if anticipating a dance from the sultry Cheyenne, who was the top billed girl in this place. He would have to cough up more than a few dubs to get a dance with her. Even if he did, that wasn't what she was here for; tonight was her night off so she had to be here to speak on this favor she wanted from me.

"Hey fellas," she greeted, giving me a church hug and a cordial kiss on the cheek. She placed a hand to her mouth in surprise and held her arms out to Vaughn, whose thirsty ass was playing it cool. Barely. "Butta? Oh shit, we got a local celebrity in here tonight. It's a pleasure to meet you."

Vaughn shot me a triumphant look over her shoulder, which I laughed at. "Nice to meet you, ma."

"I figured since I was popping in to talk business that I would bring over a bottle of the good shit, compliments of me," Cheyenne said, pouring glasses of champagne. She handed me mine and used giving Vaughn his as a cover to sit closer to him. "Maine, I need you to hook one of my girls up with a job here."

"What's wrong with her?" I asked over the flute of champagne.

Cheyenne placed a hand to her chest. "Why it gotta be something wrong with her?"

"Because you came over here with champagne to soften me up, and shorty still ain't here. She must have a butter face, which if that's the case, she can work in the kitchen or something."

"She's not ugly, Maine. She's actually quite beautiful and is as sweet as pie. Our clients would love her just for that fact."

"How's the body?"

"She just had a baby a couple weeks ago, but her snapback game is strong as fuck. She's nearly flat as a board. With the right costumes she could easily work the floor as a waitress until she's cleared to dance onstage." Cheyenne leaned in and stared into my eyes, pleading with me to give this girl a chance. "I've been training her for the past few months on how to serve drinks, and we've been working on lap dance techniques. Give her one try to impress you and then you make the call."

I cocked a brow at Cheyenne. "Why are you going so hard for shorty anyway?"

"She's a good girl in a tight spot. She needs a job to pay the bills, and I figured why not help her out? Her husband ain't shit, she's got a new mouth to feed, and both you and I know these little retail jobs ain't worth shit."

I motioned for her to grab the girl. "I know you got her hiding somewhere. Bring her out."

Cheyenne motioned to the bartender, who motioned to the hallway leading to the dressing rooms. A woman appeared, dressed in a black leather corset, fishnets, and a pair of matching boy shorts. Heads turned at her appearance, with ass men staring at the decent amount of cake poking out of her underwear and breast men taking in her breasts overflowing from the top of the corset. It was obvious she had the body for this, but I needed to see her face to figure out where I could put her. Her bone structure was delicate, her full lips inviting, and when her eyes locked with mine I was rooted to my seat.

"Nubia?"

Nubia's eyes widened and she went from being a siren to a timid mouse. Cheyenne stared between the two of us, surprised that we knew each other, while Vaughn's eyes raked Nubia over the rim of his champagne flute. I cut my eyes at him and he turned his attention back to Cheyenne, where it was safe. Of all the women that came through here looking for work, I never imagined that Nubia would be one of them. I had once told her that she was dead to me, and as much as I wanted to believe it, seeing her here and now brought those old feelings

I once had back to life.

"Hi, Maine," Nubia said, tugging at a piece of the waist length wig she wore. "I...um...I'm here to audition."

I played it cool, motioning for her to begin. Rihanna's "Work" came on and Nubia began to seductively wine to the beat, stiff at first but becoming smoother with each roll. Her eyes focused on the floor for a few beats and lifted as if pulled up by an invisible string. I sipped my champagne, enjoying this more than I thought I would. From the moment I met Nubia she always had this innocent shtick, and while I enjoyed it, seeing her embrace her inner hoe turned me on. I snapped my fingers twice, and the curtains to my section were closed. Cheyenne grabbed Vaughn by the hand and tugged him from the section, giving us the privacy I required.

"Damn," I said, reaching over and picking up the forgotten bottle of champagne and sipping on it as Nubia danced. "You gon' dance over there or come a little closer?"

Nubia spun and sat her fat ass on my lap, grinding on me without missing a beat. She leaned into me, percolating as she rubbed her breasts to Konshens' "I'm Coming." I sat back and enjoyed the show, picturing her doing all of this bouncing and grinding on my steadily throbbing dick. When the second dance was finished, I leaned in and asked, "How much to fuck?"

"What?" Nubia scrambled off of my lap, nearly breaking her neck in the six-inch pumps she wore. She turned around looking like I had actually stuck the tip in. "Cheyenne didn't mention anything about fucking."

I chuckled at the frightened look on her face. "It's a question our private dancers get on the regular. I wanted to see if you were here to sell sex or the illusion of sex."

"I'm here to pay my bills with my pussy intact," Nubia said, placing a hand on her chest to calm herself down.

I reached behind my ear and grabbed the blunt I kept there. Nubia took a seat across from me, crossing her leg and watching as I sparked up. I offered her some of the champagne, which she declined along with a pull. She sat perfectly still as if trying to will herself invisible, which was impossible to do when she had taken over the small section. The smell of her perfume permeated the air, I could still feel the heat from her body where it touched mine, and now everything in the room complimented her; the dim lighting bouncing off of her face, giving it an ethereal look, her shape making the butter leather chair she was sitting in look like a throne, and music became more palatable as she shook one of her toned legs to the beat.

"Is stripping what you really want?" I asked her after staring at her five minutes too long.

Nubia shrugged. "It's not what I want, but right now it's the only way I can make the money I need. I've tried an honest job—that didn't work. I've tried a not-so-honest job—that didn't work either. Now I need one somewhere in between."

"So you have no problem gettin' up on a stage and taking your clothes off for money? Niggas might see you on the street and dog you, these hoes in here will fuck with you if you start stealing their customers, and you gotta know your worth because these men will short you on it if you let them."

"I've already been dogged in public by my husband while fully dressed, my aunt has been fucking with me since the day I was dropped on her doorstep, and I've been shorted my entire fucking life." Nubia's bottom lip trembled, and I felt this strong urge to pull her into my arms so I can make that lip stop with my own. "I know I don't act strong, but I've been through a lot of shit in my life and I'm still here. Let me get this money, Maine."

Whether she knew it or not, Nubia was shortchanging herself. She was absolutely right—the entire world had been beating her ass for as long as she could remember—but what she deemed as not having enough strength was the exact opposite. Leaving Vincent and working as a courier was a big step, as was leaving him alone when everyone thought she would've went crawling back to him. With the birth of her child only weeks ago, I was positive that she needed every last dollar she could get, and instead of turning to Vincent, she was hustling for her own. The last time I saw her, I told her that her child didn't stand a chance, but here she was trying to create that chance the best way she could, and I couldn't knock that hunger. If a position on the pole was what she wanted, then she would have it.

"Congratulations," I said, holding the bottle of champagne out to her. "You got the job."

Nubia leapt out of her seat and straight into my arms, hugging me tight as she chanted, "Thank you, Maine." I stiffened underneath her embrace, shocked and excited by her touch. She must've taken it as something negative because she backed up and apologized profusely.

"I'm sorry about that. I'm just…happy. You ever been so happy in your life that you don't know what to do with yourself?"

I looked up at her smiling hard like she won the lottery, her excitement contagious. I had never felt that type of happiness until right now, but I knew exactly what I wanted to do: wrap her up in my arms and never let go.

"How about we celebrate with dinner?" I asked, placing my hands possessively on her waist.

Nubia stared at me in shock as her smile grew wider from her second surprise of the night. She nodded her head. "I'd…I'd like that."

"I'll pick you up tomorrow night around eight," I said, and it wasn't a question.

"What should I wear?"

I wanted to tell her whatever provided the easiest access, but I would enjoy unwrapping her like she was a present. "Put on something nice. Make sure you get your hair and nails done too," I said, reaching in my pocket and peeling off two stacks. "Is this enough?"

"I…I can't accept that," Nubia said, holding her hands in the air.

I folded the money in half and placed it in her bustier. "Consider it payment for your first dance."

"Don't set the bar too high," Nubia joked, pushing the cash down farther so no one could see it. "You'll have my head getting all big."

I raised my brows and joked back, "You keep sitting on top of me like this and you'll make mine bigger."

Nubia looked down at the position we were in. I lifted my hips a bit and she scrambled from my lap for a second time, eliciting a laugh from me. She straightened herself up and said, "I'll see you tomorrow, Maine."

I waved at her and wished her a good night, thinking to myself how it could've been a better night if I took her home with me. I rebuked the thought as soon as it came on, because whether I wanted to admit it or not, a soft spot had grown in my heart for this girl.

Nubia

*C*heyenne eyed me suspiciously as we made our way back to my place. For some reason unbeknownst to me, she didn't believe that I got the job from Maine without fucking. I wanted to share with her that we had a bit of a past, but I felt like it would be smarter to keep my cards close to my chest. What I have going on for me isn't for everyone to know. Homegirl kept pressing, and I was only able to evade the rest of her questions by promising to let her know how our dinner went tomorrow night.

"Dinner?" she said as we entered my apartment. "You mean to tell me that you did a little shimmy, popped that ass, and got a date for it? Maybe I should take some lessons from you..."

"I mean you weren't doing too bad with Butta," I said, recalling how close the two were when I emerged from my audition. "He seems pretty cool and was checking for you as we were leaving."

"He was, but I already heard from my girl that he has a side, and that bitch is territorial. His main won't even fuck with shorty. Am I looking for a come up? Yes, but not if it means fighting with some hoe and having it posted all over social media." Cheyenne started stripping from her clothes on her way to the bathroom. "I'm taking the couch tonight because the last thing I want is to be in bed with those two little girls. They sleep wild as hell."

Cheyenne and I had grown close over the past few months, with her becoming the best friend I always wanted and thought I had at one point in time. She was a hoe and had no problem letting the world know, which made it quite easy to fuck with her because if she had your man, she would tell you about it. I also loved the relationship she had with her daughter, Kiara. Like me, Cheyenne was in an abusive relationship with Kiara's father, and left him with nothing but the clothes on her back. Kiara was three at the time, but remembered those nights of sleeping in a shelter and couch hopping until Cheyenne was able to do better. They had an unbreakable bond, and it was exactly what I wanted with my baby girl, Rhea.

"Hello, angel," I said, accepting her from Donette, the young girl from across the hall I paid to watch Rhea while I ran errands. She was a stay-at-home mom with a three-year-old of her own and figured some extra cash for what she was doing anyway was better than nothing. "Hey, Donette, thanks for watching her tonight. I'm gonna need you tomorrow as well."

"You got the job?" Donette asked, leaning against the door to get all the tea. "I shouldn't be surprised, because when you left here you were looking every part of a boss bitch."

"I did get the job. Tomorrow an old friend is taking me out to celebrate."

Donette placed a hand to her chest. "A new job and reuniting with an old friend? Tonight was most definitely your night."

"It was," I replied, smiling down at a slumbering Rhea. "Well, I'll see you tomorrow."

Today had been a good day, with me stepping out in a manner I never had and building up enough confidence for Maine no matter what we had been through. Once I saw him sitting there, I was certain that he would have me kicked out of the club. However, he surprised me by allowing me to dance for him and paying me when he didn't have to. And he wants to have dinner?

"Your mama got asked on a date tonight," I told Rhea as I laid her on her side of the bed and placed the blanket up to her chest. "I haven't been on one of those since your father asked me to marry him. This guy is really nice…in an aggressive kinda way. I like him a lot, and maybe one day he'll meet you and like you."

Rhea smiled in her sleep as if she was listening. I curled up and watched her sleep, like I did every night. No matter how much dancing I did or money I made, this would always be the highlight of my night.

******

I stood in front of Silk Tresses, deciding whether or not I really wanted to go inside. On one hand, I knew I could hit up one of the local Dominican salons and get a blowout, but on the other hand, I knew Shahani would have me looking like money. I wanted to make a lasting impression on Maine, and that would require me seeing the best. I also knew it would require me facing Shahani, who I hadn't seen in nearly a year. While my life was slowly being patched together, Shahani looked like hers never fell apart. She was dressed in a Rachel leather pencil skirt with a ruffled white blouse and a pair of leather pumps on her feet. Her hair was in a halo of blonde curls, which looked good on her cinnamon colored skin. I wasn't sure how long I stood there watching, but it had to have been a while because the receptionist scared the shit out of me and caught the attention of Shahani.

"Miss, do you have an appointment today?" the receptionist asked politely, taking in the messy bun on my head.

I shook my head. "No, I don't have one, but I was hoping that you take walk-ins. I'd like to have my hair done by Shahani."

"I'm sorry, but Shahani is booked all—"

"Fill her in," Shahani interrupted as she approached. "I'll work through lunch and see if you can call my three o'clock and have her come in tomorrow. Tell her I'll discount her service as well."

The receptionist nodded her head profusely. "I'll get right on it. Cameron, can you shampoo her please?"

A young girl organizing shampoo bottles came flouncing over with a smile on her face, her pink hair bouncing with every step. Shahani placed a hand on her shoulder and said to me, "Cameron will shampoo and deep condition you, then hand you off to me. I'll see you in a few."

Shahani had come a long way from doing hair in her kitchen, and no matter what happened between the two of us, I was happy to see her living out her dream. She resumed working on her client's hair, expertly cutting the woman's hair into layers. I spent my entire shampoo contemplating what I was going to do with my hair. I had done short and found it harder to manage than when it was long. In the end, all I knew was that I wanted to look good, and that's exactly what I told Shahani once I was in her chair.

"I am going to make you look finger-licking good," she joked as she wrapped a cape around me and got to work. "We have to get rid of these ends. They're split and holding you back."

"Do what you gotta do. I've always trusted you when it comes to my hair," I said, catching the unintentional shade in my comment.

If Shahani caught it, she didn't say anything and opted to keep it cute. "You sure did. You're the only person that actually believed I could achieve this. Thank you for having more faith in me than I had in myself."

I bit my lip, unaware of how to proceed, so I settled with. "You're welcome." Pause. "I think you've always had more faith in me than I had in myself, despite past actions."

Shahani stopped combing. "I think we need to clear the air. Follow me."

I followed Shahani down the hall to a private salon area. She mentioned this was where she handled her celebrity clients whenever they came through. I watched as she set everything up, mindlessly rambling on banal topics for a few minutes. She finally stopped talking and looked at me, her expression strained as she caught sight of the blank expression on my face.

"I...I never told you about Vincent because there was no easy way to start that conversation. Was I sleeping with him? Yes, I was, and to be quite honest, I'm ashamed of it. Everything wasn't as cut and dry as Nia made it seem. I was fucking Vincent while you were dating him, but I barely knew you and on top of that, he never explicitly told me he was dating you. He started ghosting me on the regular once he got with you. I didn't find out that the two of you were in a relationship until he picked you up at the store one day."

"Even after you found out, you were still fucking him," I countered. "Smiling in my face, listening to me talk about all the nice places he was taking me, and you were fucking him all along. Why'd you even stop?"

"Because I got pregnant and Vincent…Vincent beat the baby out of me." Shahani buckled over and sobbed like a baby. "He punched me in my stomach repeatedly and I miscarried days later."

I hopped out of the salon chair and hugged her, squeezing her tight as I rocked her back and forth. I would have never imagined that the affair between Vincent and Shahani had such a tragic ending. "Why didn't you tell me? I would have left him alone, Shahani."

"I never thought in a million years that he would do you the way he did me. You were this girl he was falling in love with, and I was nothing but someone he was fucking on the low," Shahani sniffled. "He put you on a pedestal and I thought you were safe there. By the time Vincent showed his true colors, it was already too late for me to say anything without causing drama. I'm sorry for keeping it from you so long…"

"Forget about it," I said, holding her face in my hands. "Vincent did a number on me, and I can only imagine what he did to you. Did Donovan and his infidelity issues play a role in it?"

Shahani mutely nodded. "We hit hard times where I wasn't sure what the fuck I was doing with him. He was out all times of night, fucking the girls we used to keep around. I wanted a release and that's when I met Vincent. I didn't mean anything to him, I can promise you that, and I'm pretty sure that while I thought he meant something to me, he was nothing more than an opportunity to get away from my life."

"I can't believe I've been sitting here mad at you when you've been holding all of this in...lemme get you something to wipe your face with." I grabbed a few napkins from the tissue box and handed them to her. "I'm sorry for not hearing you out sooner, Shahani. I felt hurt and betrayed."

Shahani dabbed at her eyes, making sure not to ruin her perfect makeup. "I'm sorry for not being a real friend and telling you upfront. I promise to never hide anything from you ever again."

We hugged, and as much as I wanted to act like I hadn't missed anything, hugging Shahani reminded me of exactly how much I missed her. Of course I had built a bond with Cheyenne, but my issues with Shahani forced me to build up a wall and keep her at bay. With this entire ordeal behind us, I felt like I could heal and trust again. Shahani and I played catch up as she did my hair, laughing and joking like old times. I didn't mention my new job to her just yet because I didn't want her worrying about me. When she finished, I looked amazing; the four inches of dead hair I had were chopped off, leaving me with bra length hair cut in layers. Shahani topped it off by doing my makeup, creating a flawless yet natural look.

"Girl, I love it," I said, staring at myself in the mirror and for once being happy with what I saw. "I can't believe I look beautiful."

Shahani scoffed. "You've always been beautiful. I don't know who told you that you weren't, but they're obviously a hating ass hoe."

"My aunt beat it into my head and I never quite escaped it."

"Only a miserable, old, bitter bitch would mentally beat down a child. She talked all that shit to you not because you weren't beautiful, but because you were. You intimidated her and she knew that no matter how hard she tried, she could never be half as amazing as you are. Don't spend your time reliving her harsh words; pray for her and move on."

"You're right," I said, taking one last look at myself. I grabbed my purse and rummaged through it, peeling off a couple hundreds. "How much do I owe you, Shahani?"

"Not a damn thing," she said, refusing the money with a wave of her hand. "Today you've repaid me with your friendship, and that's what means the world to me right now. I haven't had a really good friend to talk to since we stopped talking and I've felt so lonely."

"Me, too. Some nights I just wanted to call you and break down, but I knew I had to keep myself together." I was placing the cash back into my purse when I caught my phone lighting up. "Hello?"

"Nubia," Maine greeted me politely, and I could hear something different in his voice. "I have to reschedule our dinner for next weekend. I had an emergency business meeting pop up, and I gotta go off the grid for a while. How does next week sound?"

I heard what sounded like a woman sobbing in the background and figured he might be having a family emergency. "Next Friday would be cool."

"Aight, see you next Friday at eight."

He hung up without another word. Shahani watched the exchange with mild concern. I eased her worries with a smile and wiggle of my phone. "Maine had to reschedule. It sounds like something came up."

"Maine? The same Maine that almost killed Vincent's grimey ass? You were going on a date with him?" Shahani giggled excitedly. "Well, if you aren't going to dinner with him tonight, then why don't I take you out? You're looking all gorgeous and that shouldn't go to waste."

I placed a hand on my chest playing coy. "Shahani, you're taking me out on a date? Bitch, I'm flattered."

She pulled me in for a playful hug. "You damn straight I am. Anything to see you smiling."

Maine

*N*iqua huffed. "So I'm a fucking business meeting? That's all I mean to you, Maine? It's bad enough you don't do nothing but treat me like shit all the time, and now I gotta hear about you making plans with a bitch? What happened to our plans? Or am I only good enough for a fuck and that's it."

"Niqua, I don't know how many times I have to explain this to you, but lemme make myself clear one more fucking time: THERE IS NO US! I come over and eat dinner, fuck you, and go about my business. I explained this from the jump, and it's like whenever you even sense there's another woman in my life you pull this bullshit."

"Because it should be me! I have held you down Maine from day one. I've been your emotional backbone, I've done runs for you when niggas would fuck up; shit, I've been trying to find this fucking girl for you for the past three months. You obviously don't need my help with that now."

I had woken up in one of the best moods I had felt in a long time. Estalita was gone for the weekend so I didn't have to worry about her calling for my whereabouts every hour. I found the perfect restaurant to take Nubia to for tonight. To top it off, I found a nice spot for us to chill at afterwards, which was never an easy feat because most of the City was overrun with tourists. Overall, my day had been running smoothly until I got a call from Niqua saying that she needed for me to come over ASAP. I was thinking maybe she had some information on the girl I was looking for, but no, all she called me over here for was some bullshit.

"Niqua, speak on what the fuck you called me here for," I barked with enough bass to have her take a few steps back.

She reached into her back pocket and pulled out a pregnancy test. "It's positive."

"Because you're positively insane," I shot back. "Every time we've fucked I used protection."

"Not every time. One time you fell asleep and woke up moaning. I comforted you and we slept together with no condom. I tried to get you to put on one, but you weren't having it—"

"Whether I strapped up or not, you told me that you were on the pill."

Niqua shrugged apologetically. "I had a tooth infection and had to take penicillin for it. I didn't know it would make the pills ineffective until it was too late..."

"Bullshit, Niqua. You're a fucking CNA. How the fuck wouldn't you know something like that?"

"I'm an RN," Niqua shot back, her expression one of hurt. "I'm a fucking RN, and I've been one since you met me, but you wouldn't know that because all you've been doing is listening long enough to fuck."

I wagged my finger at her, chuckling. "That's where you're wrong;

I haven't been listening to you at all."

"That's a real fucked up thing to say to the soon-to-be mother of your child." Niqua's chest was heaving and I could see the unshed tears in her eyes. "You know who might listen to me though? Your fiancée. You know, the one you're marrying in a matter of weeks."

I pulled out my phone and pulled up Estalita's contact information. "You wanna call Estalita and let her know you're pregnant? Go ahead. By the end of the night she'll have you gutted and melting in a vat of acid. Mamí is cartel, and you sleeping on that pretty face will have you wiped off the fucking map."

This conversation wasn't going how Niqua wanted, and I could practically see the wheels churning behind her eyes as she tried to think of her next route. She opted for the obvious: tears. I ran a hand through my hair as I tried to figure out how to calm this girl down long enough to leave five stacks for her to handle her business.

"Niqua," I said, watching as she kneeled over on her bed and rocked herself from side to side. I took two steps towards her, reaching my hand out like I was getting ready pet a rabid dog when Niqua bolted upright pointing a gun at me. "Yo, what the fuck is wrong with you? Put that fucking gun down before you hurt yourself."

Niqua shook her head profusely. "I'm not putting down a motherfucking thing. You think you can walk over me without any consequences? That's not how this works, Jermaine."

I leaned in and stopped when the barrel of the gun touched my forehead. "If you bold enough to pull a muhfuckin' gun on me, then you better be brave enough to pull the trigger, bitch."

"Maine—"

"You better lay me the fuck out, Niqua. Shoot me right between the eyes."

"Maine, I—"

"Pull the fucking trigger!"

"I didn't mean it like—"

"PULL THE FUCKING TRIGGER BITCH!"

Niqua buckled, lowering the gun and sobbing into her hands. I straightened up and headed for the door before I fucked up and did something stupid like blow this bitch's brains out. I had my hand on the knob when she shouted, "Maine, if you leave I'll kill myself. Blow my head right off of my shoulders."

I turned around and saw Niqua sitting there with the gun pointed into the bottom of her throat. I was willing to bet my last dime that she had the safety on and was pulling another one of her stunts. I was sick and tired of her presenting me with these empty ass ultimatums, so I called her on her bluff and replied, "Do it."

The sound of the gunshot was deafening. I jumped as Niqua's head bucked as the back of it was blown off. Her body fell off the bed, crumbling in a heap. I leaned against the doorway and closed my eyes as a childhood memory was triggered.

******

It was a peaceful night in the forest, one of the first we'd had in a long time. The balmy air tickled my skin as I lay on my back watching the night sky. It was moments of divine silence where I would think of my family. Every night I prayed they were okay, but for the past few nights I had been experiencing this sinking feeling in the pit of my stomach. It had intensified to the point where it made me sick. I spent the better part of the day pushing it down deep inside as we traveled through the forest preparing for our next attack. We had been successful, and with this victory under our belt we were given one celebratory night. As Foday and the other boys smoked and drank around the fire, I stayed to myself. My thoughts flickered from my mother to my little sister, Siabanda, and my little brother, Babah. My father was killed when Babah was a baby, leaving me to become the man of the house. I was in the middle of praying for them when Foday shook me out of my trance, his expression grim.

"They destroyed Freetown," Foday said. "Burned it to the ground. There are very few left."

I blinked, my expression remaining blank as if I hadn't heard that the town I grew up in had been destroyed, and the chances of my family still being alive were slim to none. Foday studied me, waiting for some kind of reaction, and when he didn't receive one, he offered me a beer. I accepted the warm bottle, guzzling down its contents in a few quick gulps. Sensing that I wanted to be alone, Foday went back to the group. When I was sure that no one was paying attention to me, I dipped into the pitch black forest. I stopped when I could no longer hear their laughs. My hand blindly searched my waist for my gun. It was a gift from the general, who recognized me for my hard work out in the trenches.

Silent tears rolled down my cheeks as I placed the barrel of the pistol into my mouth, the taste of ash and dirt settling on my tongue. If I pulled the trigger, I knew I could be with my family again and free of the war. I thought of the people I had killed in cold blood, and considered the fact that I might not end up with my family after all. The only way I would know was if I pulled the trigger. Taking a steadying breath, I relaxed and prepared myself for death. My hand wrapped around the trigger, and I squeezed.

******

I woke up in a sweaty heap, chest heaving as I tried to make sense of my surroundings. You would think that after seven days of repeating the same dream I would be used to it by now, but there was nothing familiar about the feeling. Ever since I watched Niqua blow her brains out, I had been blowing my own out in my sleep for the past week. She didn't mean much to me, but I never would've imagined that Niqua and I would've come to an end with her splattered all over her bedroom wall. I wasn't sure how long I stood in the doorway staring at her, but I snapped out of my trance long enough to get out of her apartment before the cops showed up. I didn't doubt that her neighbors heard us arguing and called the cops once that fatal shot was fired. I was right; on my way out the cops were speeding to her apartment. I went home and washed off the night, or at least I thought I did until I woke up hours later, reliving one of the lowest points of my life. I pushed it back into the compartment I kept it in while I was on my grind, but the moment I sparked up a blunt and slipped into a peaceful slumber, I was back in Sierra Leone facing my inner demons.

"Baby, what's wrong?" Estalita asked as I passed her on my way to the bathroom to shower. "Jermaine!"

I ignored her, in no mood to answer any of her prying questions.

She knew something was wrong but knew better than to ask exactly what. Or at least I thought she did.

"You've been screaming in your sleep," Estalita said, after barging into the bathroom and watching me brush my teeth. "Screaming 'Foday.' Who's 'Foday'?"

"None of your fucking business," I snapped, spitting toothpaste into her face.

She wiped it away with a trembling hand. "It's my business when I have to answer phone calls from the front desk making sure that everything is okay, because people keep thinking I'm up here killing you."

"Next time they call put me on the phone; I'll tell them to mind their fucking business, too. Better yet, I'll let them know personally when I'm on my way out."

Estalita regretted spilling the beans. "Maine, please don't go down there and embarrass me."

"If I'm such an embarrassment, then why are we even doing this? Why you fucking with me if I'm embarrassing? What, you got so desperate to get from under your father that any nigga will do?" When she didn't reply back, I knew where I stood with her, and it made whatever pinch of guilt I had for cheating on her, evaporate. "Good to fucking know."

"Don't act like you aren't with me for the same reason. Me and my family are the closest you will ever come to greatness," Estalita shot back, her nostrils flaring. "You promised me the world, and now I'm starting to feel like it was only to get into my pants. I'm tired of trying to knock down the wall you have built up, and I'm starting to think that maybe we rushed into this."

I went back to brushing my teeth, allowing my silence to answer the question. Like any woman, Estalita could dish it but she certainly couldn't take it. She sucked in her lower lip and stormed out of the bathroom, slamming the door behind her. The only plus side to her not speaking to me, was that it gave me the silence I craved. I was able to shower, shave, and line myself up in peace. Estalita watched me picking out my outfit for the night from the privacy of the pillow fortress she made in our California king bed. I decided on a Kiton suit I had made quite a while ago for random business meetings. It was tailored to perfection, giving my slim yet muscular build the right silhouette. My Louboutin loafers; Thomas Pink shirt, tie, and pocket square; Cartier tie clip, and matching cuff links set the entire look off. Two sprays of my Tom Ford cologne had her sniffing the air as I walked past her.

"Good night to you, too," she muttered from the protection of the blankets.

It was going to be a good night. If there was one person that could take my mind off of the events of last week, it would be Nubia and that beautiful smile of hers.

******

I watched Nubia with mild amusement. For someone that grew up in New York City, she was infatuated with everything we passed. The busy streets of the Lower East Side, the clothing stores in Soho, and the partygoers all through Union Square. I was starting to think if I should've taken her on a bus tour or something. If I thought that interest was something, she lit up as we entered Times Square. This place was hated by all native New Yorkers and I had an aversion to it as well, but in order for me to get to the spot we were having dinner at, I had to go through this circus. I was cussing out yellow cabs and obnoxious ass pedestrians when I heard Nubia sigh wistfully.

"I've always wanted to see *The Lion King*. My aunt would go every year with my uncle and cousin, but they'd leave me behind. One day I'm going to go and watch it in the best seats in the theater," she said resolutely as she stared up at the sign for the Broadway show.

I made a sharp turn, ignoring the honking of the cars and the cuss words of those who I had nearly run over in my haste to get into the left lane so I could turn. Nubia looked at me like I had lost my mind, her eyes widening in shock before it turned to excitement.

"Are we going where I think we're going?" she asked with a hint of excitement in her voice.

I pulled up to the parking garage and waited for the valet to come and grab my keys. "You said you wanted to see The Lion King, right?"

"Yeah..."

"Well then that's what we gon' do."

Nubia lit up like Christmas had come early. She was talking a mile a minute about how *The Lion King* was her favorite movie growing up. It was mine as well, and I would never admit it to anyone, but I had cried when Mufasa died. This was during a brighter time of my life, when I was still an innocent little kid, but the loss still resonated within me because I had lost my own father.

"Good evening," I said to the ticket agent. "I'd like two of the best seats in the house."

"What?" Nubia yelped.

I kept strong eye contact with the agent so she knew better than to second-guess me, and my spending capabilities. She clicked on her keyboard for a few minutes and announced, "Your total will be $542.13." She accepted the business Amex I handed her and replied, "Thank you."

Nubia stood excitedly by my side, her eyes lighting up in delight when the woman handed me back my card and our orchestra seat tickets. I guided her upstairs to where they were serving refreshments and kept the gift store. I didn't even think twice as I pulled her over to the small store and told the cashier to give me one of everything.

"It's always crazy when the show lets out," I told Nubia as the cashier started making a small stockpile of merchandise. I picked up the charm bracelet and popped it out of its box, placing it on Nubia's slender wrist. I fingered the tiny wooden charms as I stared deep into her eyes. "It ain't diamonds, but I don't want you to think of diamonds when you think of me. There's nothing remotely perfect about me or my situation. But I am a warrior made of wood that will always be here whenever you need me."

Nubia placed her hand on top of mine and replied, "You always are, even when I don't deserve it."

The cashier returned with all of our items, interrupting the bonding moment with her chattering. I took Nubia's hand into mine and gave it a gentle squeeze. She smiled back at me and I felt this weird churning in my stomach. I thought it might've had something to do with what I ate last night, but then I considered that it might be those butterflies I always heard people talking about.

******

"That was so amazing," Nubia gushed as we cruised down Sixth Avenue. "I knew I was going to like it, but I didn't think I would fall in love. Maine, that was amazing. Thank you for taking me to see *The Lion King*. I'll never forget it."

She was smiling at me with those perfect teeth of hers, and I couldn't help but to smile back. "I'm happy you enjoyed it."

"Did I?"

Nubia recapped the entire play and gave her commentary on it. I found myself chuckling at her goofy ass once she started singing "Hakuna Matata." We were in high spirits once we pulled up to the restaurant. My appetite returned somewhere around act two, and I was starving. Nubia mentioned the same, noting that she had been so nervous all she ate today was a peach.

"It was a good peach but I'm still—where is everyone?"

Instead of taking Nubia to a restaurant filled with noisy ass people and bland food, I rented out a recently closed down restaurant and found a chef that specialized in West African cooking. He and his team had spent all day today whipping up a feast of Sierra Leonean dishes, and a few American ones in case Nubia didn't take to the spices and flavors. It would be just the two of us for the night, getting to know each other without the drama from both our sides.

"It's just us," I said, taking a seat at the perfectly set table.

Nubia glanced around excitedly. "What are we eating?"

"West African cuisine, specifically Sierra Leonean cuisine."

"Is that where you're from?" Nubia asked with keen interest. "Whenever you're mad you sound like a totally different person."

It was true; I had been living in NYC for ten years and learned to turn off my accent quite easily, but once I was riled up, I dropped the façade and went back to my roots. "Yes, I was born and raised there until I was fifteen."

"Did you come here with your parents?"

I shook my head. "My entire family is dead."

"So is mine," Nubia said, her eyes growing a little shiny. "So... what are we eating tonight?"

The conversation became much lighter, with me giving her a breakdown of customs when it came to eating food from my country. Our first dish was brought out and Nubia adapted easily, using bread and her fingers to pick up her food. I told Nubia about my childhood before the war and she listened intently. She told me stories from her childhood as well, and judging by some of them, she didn't grow up with the humble beginnings that most of us did. She told stories of visiting London, France, and multiple islands in the Caribbean. I was shocked when she mentioned that she was given a pony for her seventh birthday.

"I haven't talked about these memories in a really long time," she admitted, her voice growing thick. "I kinda pushed them deep down inside after my parents were killed. When I was little, I would use them to get me through rough times, but after a while I stopped, because I knew no matter how much I daydreamed, they weren't coming back. I started associating those memories with pain and knew I couldn't keep pulling myself back into the past."

"I've blocked it all out, but every once in a blue my sister's smiling face invades my dreams, and I just…"

I didn't have to finish the sentence because Nubia nodded her head in understanding. A buzzing came from her purse and she pulled out her phone, mentioning that it could've been her babysitter. I was getting ready to crack on her ass for still walking around with an Obama phone in 2017 when I saw the smile on her face drop. She threw her phone back into her purse and buried her face in her hands. She emerged a minute later visibly upset.

"Speaking of a memory I didn't want to relive, my aunt just texted me 'Happy Birthday.'" She shook her head. "I will never understand how some people can be so fucking evil. She knows my birthday is a sore spot for me."

"You wanna talk about it?"

Nubia shook her head as she held back tears. "No, I just wanna get out of here. I'm not hungry anymore."

I personally thanked the chef for a wonderful dinner and we headed out. Nubia leaned her head against the window, staring blankly ahead. I had reached the FDR Drive when Nubia placed her hand on mine and said, "I don't wanna go home."

I changed lanes and headed for the Jersey Turnpike. I hadn't been back to my old place in a while and knew the solitude was exactly what Nubia needed. Although I didn't enjoy any of the amenities because I stayed in the streets, I was positive that Nubia would enjoy the whirlpool bathtub, fireplace, terrace overlooking the city, and fully stocked kitchen with enough ice cream flavors to compete with Baskin Robbins.

"This place is amazing," she said, shrugging out of her coat. "How long have you been living here?"

"A couple years," I replied, accepting her coat and getting a good look at her wearing the fuck out of the black velvet dress hugging her curves. "I just finished decorating it a few months ago."

Nubia traveled deeper into the house, taking in the warrior art that dotted my walls. "You did a really good job."

"Make yourself at home," I told her as I made my way down the hall to my bedroom.

The maid I hired to come through here once a week and dust had been doing her job. She even changed the covers, although my California king hadn't been slept in since last year. I entered the bathroom and drew Nubia a bath. While the water was running, I grabbed her a T-shirt and pair of shorts to sleep in. I came out of the closet and found Nubia sitting on my bed. Those curious hands of hers traveled over the bedroom as she tried to get a read on the type of person I was, based on my room. Too bad for her that I wasn't too fond of personal effects.

"I drew you a bath," I told her as I placed the tee and shorts in her hand. "Relax, get your mind together, and have a good night. I'll be in the guest room if you need me."

Nubia bit her lip as if she wanted to say something, but settled with, "Thank you, Maine."

I saluted her and headed to the guestroom, where I hopped into the shower, allowing the twelve simultaneous jets of water to knead my tense muscles, relaxing me for what might be the best night's sleep I had in a long time. I lay on top of the silk sheets in nothing but my towel, allowing the cool air to lull me into a peaceful rest. I was halfway there when the bedroom door opened and Nubia appeared. She climbed into bed with me, settling herself underneath the sheets.

"I didn't wanna be by myself," she explained. "I hope you don't mind."

"No," I said, peering over at her. I slung my arm around her and pulled her close.

She sank into my embrace, nuzzling into the crook of my neck and slinging an arm across my chest. I drifted asleep once again, and was nearly there when I felt a pair of soft lips press against mine. My eyes popped open and there was Nubia, hovering over me as she gauged my reaction. *How the fuck did she manage to get on top of me?* I thought as my hands traced over her thick thighs.

"You forgot to give me my kiss goodnight," she reminded me. "So I figured I would take it."

"Word?" I laughed.

She nodded her head vigorously. "Yup."

I sat up without moving my hands from her waist until she was sitting in my lap and kissed her with authority. She melted in my arms, pressing her body against mine as I tongued her ass down. Her hands grabbed ahold of my back, numbing everywhere they touched, like

Novocain. A startled moan escaped her lips, and I wasn't sure what brought it on until I felt my dick pressing against the inside of her leg.

"You don't have to do nothing you don't want to, but I'm not gon' lie—A nigga can't sleep in the same bed as you and keep his hands to himself," I told her after a minute.

Nubia weighed her options and replied, "Then don't."

I flipped her onto her back in one fluid movement. Nubia stared up at me in nervous anticipation, and had she not given birth to a child, I would've thought she was a virgin. I slid the basketball shorts off of her and was greeted by her pretty pussy. I spread her legs, watching her get wet for me. She tasted as good as she looked, and I took my time enjoying her. Nubia clenched the sheets as I sucked and swirled my tongue around her sensitive clit.

"Mai...ooh...fuck," she moaned as I slipped my tongue into her, fucking her relentlessly. She tried crawling away, and I pulled her right back, lapping up the juices I almost missed. "Ohmygod. I think there's something wrong..."

I slipped a finger into her, making a come here motion until she came, shaking and stuttering. She was panting like she had just ran a marathon, and little did baby girl know, we were just getting started. I planted a gentle trail of kisses up her body, tasting the light sheen of sweat that came with a good nut, and finally made it to her quivering lips.

"What was that?" she asked, staring up at me like I had three heads.

"You've never had an orgasm?" She shook her head. "Well get

ready for another one."

I plunged deep inside of her, nearly busting off the way her walls clung to my dick like a second skin. I bit her neck to keep from groaning as she ground her hips against mine. If being around her was intoxicating, then diving into Nubia's sweet pussy would have me overdosing soon enough. Once I gained my composure, I began deep stroking, loving the way she moaned my name each time I dove in. The pace intensified, with little shy Nubia disappearing and being replaced by a woman that knew what she wanted.

"Let me ride you, Daddy," she panted, biting my lower lip as I pounded her.

I obliged her, relaxing on my back as she climbed on top and rode me like she was in the Kentucky derby. She was staring down at me with a wicked smile on her face because she knew I was whipped, and would be cumming in a minute. One slap on her fat ass had the playing field even, with her trembling under my touch, and screaming for me to slap it again. I grabbed ahold of her hair and thrust my hips to meet hers until we came together. Nubia collapsed on top of my chest where I cradled her, smoothing her hair and dotting her neck with kisses.

As we lay in bed, spent from one of the most intense fuck sessions I'd ever had, Nubia finally decided to open up to me.

"The reason why I hate my birthday so much is because it's the day my parents were killed," she admitted. "Right in front of my eyes."

"Damn, that's cold," I said, running my hands through her hair.

"Everything was so perfect that day. My mom had spent months planning my tenth birthday party. It was princess themed and everything was pink and white, including the huge castle birthday cake she had made."

I faltered in stroking her hair for a minute. "For real?"

"Yeah. We even dressed up like royalty for the day. My parents were the king and queen and I was their princess. Daddy wasn't going for having to dress in a white tux, but one look at my face and he melted.

"Everything was going just fine when gunshots started popping and people began dropping. I watched as everyone I knew and loved was butchered. Classmates, teachers, friends, and a couple of my dad's cousins. My daddy always stayed strapped, but for that day my mother told him to leave the streets at home. We were in a nice neighborhood so there was very little chance of something popping off. That assurance, that cockiness that no one would ever think to come for Apollo Monroe's family, was the reason for its destruction.

"They killed my mother first. Dragged her across the dead bodies of her friends and family. Shot her right in the head. I didn't even have a chance to say goodbye to her. Then there was my daddy. All I had time to do was tell my daddy I loved him before he was killed too. The killer was going to kill me next, but I asked him not to. For some reason unbeknownst to me, he spared my life."

The reason I spared her was because I thought of my own little sister who probably begged for her life before the rebels killed her. Nubia was the same age Siabanda would've been had she survived the Freetown Massacre, and I knew I couldn't put a bullet in her now. I decided to wait until she was older and handle my unfinished business, except now I knew it couldn't happen.

"He spared you because this world needs a beautiful person like you," I said, giving her a gentle squeeze.

I was playing a dangerous game with my gun and my heart, choosing Nubia over a pledge I made to Sampson. It was a dangerous gamble, but if I played my cards right, I could come out on top.

Nubia

I was smiling from ear-to-ear when I arrived home. My night with Maine had been everything I dreamed for and more. He went out of his way to make me feel like a princess, and it wasn't to soften me up to get whatever he wanted and bounce. I lifted the three tote bags filled with all of my Lion King merchandise higher up on my shoulders as I fished for my keys. I wanted to square everything away and grab Rhea from Donette. I checked in on her while I was at Maine's place taking a bath, and it was the only way I could rest easy.

"Someone had a nice date," Cheyenne noted from the couch where her, Kiara, and Marlee sat watching a Disney Channel movie. "Oooooh, a Broadway show? Fancy, fancy."

"Did you bring us anything, Nubia?" Marlee asked, hopping up from her seat and padding over to rummage through my bags. "Can I have this teddy bear?"

"Yes, you can," I said, rummaging through the bag and pulling out another Simba doll for Kiara. "I got you one too, baby doll."

"Say 'Thank you' to Nubia for thinking of you while she was out on her date," Cheyenne said as she snacked on her popcorn. "Because if I was out with a nigga like Maine these little ones would be the last thing on my mind."

"Girl, shut up," I joked as I handed Kiara her doll.

"Thank you, Nubia."

"You are so welcome, sweetie," I said accepting her hug and making my way into my bedroom. "Now if you'll excuse me, I'm gonna take a quick shower so I can relieve Donette of Rhea."

I undressed quickly, excited to see my baby girl after spending our first night apart. I hadn't started at the club yet, and I could only imagine the separation anxiety I would feel once I had to leave her five nights a week. In the short amount of time we spent together, Rhea had become my world, and I knew now how my parents must've felt. The only troubling part of parenting I feared was explaining to her why her father wasn't in her life. I was sitting on the edge of my bed thinking about the last time Vincent and I had spoken, when I felt my phone buzz in my coat pocket.

"Hello?"

"Nubia, how are you?"

I stared at my phone and placed it back to my ear. "Vincent?"

"Yeah, who else was you looking to call you?"

"No one," I replied, placing my hand against my chest to calm my wildly beating heart. "But since the last time I spoke to you and you wished death upon my daughter and me, I figured the next time I would see you would be in divorce court."

"You put me on the spot. I was still mad at you about letting that punk ass nigga kidnap me and try to kill me. I shouldn't have disrespected you the way I did and I'm sorry. Do you think we can link up and talk?"

I looked at my phone again. Vincent sorry? "I'll think about it."

"Nubia—."

"Vincent, that's all I can do right now. Do you know what I went through to make sure I had what I needed for our daughter when she was born? It's fucked up that you think you can just waltz back into our lives after leaving us to struggle."

"And that's why I'm trying to have a sit down with you to see where we can go from here. You're still my wife, and no matter how much you might think you control when I see my daughter, you don't. I'll go to court if I have to."

"Go ahead," I countered. "Go and explain how you abandoned both of us when we needed you the most. Explain that you weren't even there for Rhea's birth."

I could tell that Vincent was doing his best to hold on whatever anger he had, but I was on a roll and didn't plan on calming down any time soon. "Listen, Nubia. All I want is to sit down and talk to you for five, ten minutes tops about us coming together to raise our daughter. I ain't wanna involve the courts, but I will if I have to."

"Fine," I relented. "I'll come and talk to you for five minutes, but only under one condition: you have some pampers, wipes, and formula handy. If you want my time you're gonna have to pay for it."

"Whatever. How about we meet at noon at Target? I'll buy you the stuff you need for the baby, we talk, and go our separate ways."

I glanced over at the small stockpile of diapers and wipes I had for Rhea. At the rate she was going, she would need more diapers in a few days, plus I could use some extra formula. "Fine. I'll see you at one."

An hour later I was fully dressed and ready to go out and meet this trifling ass nigga. Cheyenne noticed my change in clothes and asked me where I was going.

"To meet up with Vincent's bitch ass to discuss our next steps," I said, crossing my arms. "Can you do me a favor and watch Rhea? Donette has had her since last night and I'm sure she could use a break."

"Of course I can watch her. I would've watched her last night had you asked me. Lemme wash my hands and get ready," Cheyenne said, disappearing into the kitchen.

Donette was full of smiles when I went over to her apartment. Her son was sleeping quietly as she played with Rhea, who was up gurgling. I took my baby girl into my arms and covered her with air kisses.

"She's the sweetest little baby. I had so much fun with her," Donette said as she walked us to the door. "Don't be afraid to bring her back."

I reached into my pocket and gave her the $200 I put aside for this date night. "Here you go, girl."

"Nubia, this is too much—"

"No, it's not." I slapped the money into her hand and squeezed it. "I was once a stay-at-home wife and I felt like I wasn't bringing much to the table because I wasn't making any money of my own. Take this and show hubby that you're a hustler, too."

Donette choked up a little; I could tell that she had the same fear me and other stay-at-home moms had every once in a while. "Thank you, Nubia."

After everything I had been through, it only felt right to pay it forward to another young girl navigating life the best she could. I wasn't fully rebuilt, and some days I could barely look at myself in the mirror, but now every day was worth waking up and living. I had a job opportunity to make my own money, a beautiful daughter, and a blossoming relationship with Maine. My life was coming together, and for the first time since my parents died, I had something to smile about.

I was happy.

******

I stared at my watch for the third time in ten minutes. I had been standing around the baby section of Target waiting for Vincent for the past thirty minutes. His apartment was only twenty minutes from here, so I was finding it hard to believe that traffic was holding him up. No, this nigga was just playing games as usual. I don't even know why I fed into his bullshit and agreed to meet up with him. Probably because part of me believed that although he was a terrible husband to me, he might be a decent father to our child. I guess I was wrong. It wouldn't be the first time.

"Excuse me, miss, can I interest you in signing up for a new iPhone 8?" one of the Target Mobile employees asked as I passed him on my way to the escalators. "Don't even front; I saw you using that Assurance phone."

I stuck my tongue at him. "So what? I'mma support my president's legacy till the day I die."

"I understand that, but as fine as you are, you need a phone up to par," the guy said with a shrug of his shoulders. "Lemme hook you up, ma. I even got special pricing since you're obviously a new customer."

I stared down at my phone and thought of all the people that had this number and all the bullshit they brought with them. Vivica's evil ass. Ashanti's trifling ass used to call breathing over the phone but was too dumb to block her number. Then there was Vincent, who obviously didn't give a fuck about me. Shit, he upgraded his phone multiple times while we lived together and never once thought to add me to his line. *That would've been another way to control me anyway*, I thought as I flipped the phone up and down in my hand. It was time for a change.

"You know what? Lemme get a look at that iPhone 8."

Thirty minutes later I walked out of Target with a brand new phone in hand. I saved Shahani, Maine, Cheyenne, and Donette's numbers and said to hell with the rest. I tossed my Assurance phone in the trash and headed home with a smile on my face. I would text everyone tomorrow from my phone so I could fully enjoy their reactions to my messages popping up in blue instead of green. I spent the bus ride home surfing the internet and listening to songs on YouTube. I didn't have a debit card yet so I couldn't download any apps, but I was handling that early tomorrow morning. I couldn't even lie—I now understood why Shahani was so into her phone. There was so much going on in the world: war, celebrity gossip, and lots of ratchet drama. I was still engrossed in my phone when I entered the house.

"No wonder you haven't been answering any of my calls; you bossed up and got a new phone," Cheyenne joked. "You could've called a bitch and let her know. I was gonna ask you to grab a pie for dinner."

"I still can," I said with my hand on the doorknob. "How about I have it delivered?"

"Whatever works for you, boo," Cheyenne said as she switched Rhea to her other hand. "Make sure they come all the way upstairs too; it's too cold to be going downstairs."

"Of course."

I called the pizza shop and changed into a pair of sweats along with an oversized white tee. I was heading into the living room to grab Rhea when I heard the locks turn. Myrna appeared with a wide smile on her face. Being that I hadn't seen her the entire weekend, I smiled right back, glad to know she was okay. However, my smile dropped when I saw that she wasn't alone.

"Nubia, I was coming into the building and ran into your husband. Why didn't you mention that you were married?" she asked, motioning to Vincent, who stood behind her smiling.

I took a step back. "Because we're over. Myrna, get away from him he's—Vincent!"

Vincent grabbed Myrna by the back of her neck and shoved her deeper into the house. Cheyenne and the girls made a break for my bedroom. Vincent tried to make a grab for Cheyenne but was blocked by Myrna.

"Put the fucking phone down," Vincent said, motioning to the phone clutched in my hand. "PUT THE FUCKING PHONE DOWN BEFORE I SNAP HER NECK!"

The phone hit the floor with a thud. "Leave her the fuck alone, Vincent. She has nothing to do with this."

"I'll let her go when you give me my daughter. Tell that bitch in there to dress her, pack her bag, put her important papers in it, and give her to me. If you don't, then I'll snap this crackhead's neck clean off her fucking shoulders."

I shook my head. "You're an abusive bastard, but there ain't no way in hell you would kill an innocent person and think I'mma let you walk out of here with my child." Vincent brandished a knife and placed it underneath Myrna's throat. "If you kill her, then you have to kill all of us, and that isn't happening. Let her go and we can talk."

Vincent shoved Myrna into the adjacent wall, knocking her clean out. She lay in a crumbled heap, a groan escaping her lips. I covered my mouth to keep a sob from escaping. Vincent advanced, his knife gripped tightly in his hand. This is what our relationship had come down to: neither of us could live if the other survived.

"Get in that fucking room and pack up my daughter so I can take her," Vincent said, raising his knife and pointing it at the door behind him.

I shook my head. "You're gonna have to fucking kill me."

Like any woman beater, Vincent didn't hesitate to cock his fist back and swing. I was expecting it and ducked back before his fist could connect. He lost his footing by missing me, which gave me a moment of opportunity to attack. I hit him with a mean right hook and kicked the knife he was holding right out of his hand. My victory was short-lived when he grabbed me by the neck, lifted me into the air, and slammed me into the floor. My ears rung, my vision blurred, and I almost forgot where I was. My eyes focused and I caught Vincent making his way to my bedroom door. I scooted forward and tripped him, sending him toppling to the ground.

"I told you that you gotta kill me, bitch!" I screamed, scrambling to my feet.

They barely planted when Vincent tackled me like a linebacker, sending both of us toppling into the entertainment center. Books, DVDs, and pictures flew everywhere. I hit the floor once again and felt the air leave my lungs as Vincent landed on top of me. I choked, hungry and scraping for air, as he punched me repeatedly in the face. When he grew bored of hitting me he resorted to choking.

"You really thought you could beat me, didn't you?" Vincent asked as he strangled me. "When I met you, you was nothing but a weak little bitch, and now you're gonna die like one. I won't tell my baby shit about your punk ass. She got a whole new Mommy waiting downstairs."

At the mention of Rhea growing up not knowing who I was, I felt a surge of strength. I felt my surroundings for something, anything, to hit this nigga and get him off of me. My hand tightened around his blade, and I plunged it into his neck. Vincent's eyes widened in horror as he choked to death on his own blood. He let go of my neck and held on to his own for dear life. I shoved him off of me and gasped for a breath of fresh air.

"How does it feel to be the weak one?" I asked him as I pulled the knife from his neck. "Huh? You're scared, aren't you? You should be fucking scared you punk bitch!"

Vincent started crawling away with the little bit of strength he had, leaving an ugly trail of blood behind him. I crawled to him and plunged the knife into his chest. He wheezed one final time, and his eyes widened in shock. His grip on his neck slackened and his head rolled to the side. I should've stopped there, but I was shaking with anger. Had I not stood up for myself, this would've been me. I ripped the knife from his chest and plunged it in again. And again. And again. And—

"Oh my God, what did you do to him?" a woman screamed from the front doorway followed by that familiar, "FREEZE! DROP YOUR WEAPON!"

I raised my hands in the air at the sight of the police with their weapons drawn. They converged on me before the knife could even hit the floor. My bedroom door opened and Cheyenne started yelling at them.

"What the fuck are you doing to her!" she screamed, attempting to run up on the officers that had pinned me to the ground and were tightly wrapping those cold cuffs around my wrists. "She's the victim! Uncuff her right now! Nubia, I'mma get you out of this, I promise!"

"Go in my phone and call the number labeled 'Shahani,'" I said as I was dragged from the apartment.

My adrenaline was still pumping, making everyone go in slow motion. As we grew closer to the door I instantly recognized the screaming woman as Francesca. She covered her mouth and silently cried at the sight of Vincent's body.

"You killed him," she said between sobs. "You killed him."

I laughed at the audacity of this bitch. "It was kill or be killed, bitch. If I had to, I'd do it all over again."

Shahani

This couldn't be right.

There was no way in hell this could be correct.

I sat staring at the numbers for my shop for the past thirty minutes, wondering why they were so off. I wasn't the greatest at math by a long shot, but working at KFC taught me how to balance my points to stay on budget for the month. By the first year, I had it down to an art form, which was why these mistakes made stood out so much. Sampson's accountant was fucking up, and her fuckups would have me caught by the IRS when it came time for filing. I was lucky to have caught it a month before filing began. I called Sampson to ask him about the situation, and all he told me was to come home so we could talk about it.

"What is there to talk about?" I said, slapping the ledger on the kitchen island. "Your accountant fucked up my books and she needs to unfuck them up. Everything is marked up. Do you know how many heads would have to roll through my shop for me to make this much bank? We're not doing bad for our first year, but we aren't doing this well."

Sampson flipped the ledger open and checked the numbers. His brows furrowed at the outrageous numbers like it should, but when he opened his mouth he had the audacity to say, "You're right; she fucked

180

this up really bad. It shouldn't be this visible. I'll have my girl that does my books at the construction site handle this."

"What?" I couldn't believe this. "You knew she was cooking my books and you didn't bother to tell me? I'm in charge of this business, Sampson. If something goes wrong I'll be held accountable for it."

"I wouldn't let anything happen to you," Sampson said dismissively. "Has anything happened so far? I said I would get my other girl to fix the fucking books. What more do you want?"

"I want you to stop laundering money through my shop," I said, wiping away the tears flooding my eyes, blurring Sampson and everything around me. "I'm tired of being caught in the middle of some shit. First I was in the life, and now I'm in the game?"

Sampson came around the island like a panther, his eyes never leaving mine as he backed me against it. "Yes, you are in the game. When you met me you knew I was a street nigga. You never complained when you were accepting clothes, shoes, and expensive getaways. How do you think all that shit gets paid for? With clean money. The same clean money that goes through your shop. You can get with the program or you can get the fuck out of my house and go back to your pimp—I mean ex. It's your choice."

I hung my head to keep him from seeing the tears in my eyes. "Can you just make sure it's fixed? Tax season is next month and I don't wanna get caught up."

"I can do that," Sampson said, placing his hands on my shoulders. "Now give me some sugar." I lifted my head with my eyes closed so the tears could stop falling. Samson kissed each of them and my lips. "Why don't you draw yourself a bath? When you're finished, I'll have dinner set out and ready for you. What do you want me to order?"

"I could go for some soul food," I said as I slipped past him.

"Well when you're done you'll have a feast waiting for you."

"Okay, babe."

I climbed the stairs two at a time, taking deep, calming breaths. Once I was in the privacy of the bathroom with the water running, I broke down and cried, sobbing and slobbing. I hadn't cried this hard since my mother died and I was left all alone in the world. That loneliness crept back in once again. No matter how much I tried to find a man to do right by me, they all ended up playing me. Donovan had the same drive as Alonzo, but he was too stupid and greedy. Sampson has the power Alonzo had, but he doesn't have his heart. I missed my man, and came to the realization that there would never be another Lonzo in my life. If I couldn't have my soul mate, then I might as well settle for the luxury of being Sampson's woman, no matter how empty it made me feel from time to time.

"Get over it, Shahani," I said, grabbing a handful of the warm water and splashing it on my face. "This is the best it's gonna get, boo."

I climbed to my feet and began to strip. I kicked my shoes off, unbuckled my pants, and shrugged out of my jacket. I almost tossed it when I remembered my phone was in my pocket. I pulled it out and noticed a few missed calls from a foreign number, along with a couple voicemails. I was getting ready to call it back when my phone lit up with another number from someone all too familiar.

"Nia, what the fuck do you want?" I asked with no greeting

whatsoever. "Whatever Donovan has done to you, you deserve it."

Nia sobbed into the phone. "Shahani…I really need you. I knew he had some temper issues, but I had no idea that they were this bad. I'm scared, and I can't call the cops because once he gets out, it's over for me. I need someone to talk him off the ledge. Please help me, Shahani. Please."

As much as I wanted to leave Nia's fast ass to her karma, I knew my mother would roll over in her grave. Nia's own mother ain't give a fuck about her, which was probably why the poor girl didn't know a damn thing about loyalty. I would save her ass from Donovan, but there was no way in hell I was bringing her home with me. She would get a couple weeks in a motel, and after that she was on her own.

"Where you going?" Sampson asked as I entered the kitchen to grab my car keys.

I made a random hand motion and said, "I just gotta make a quick run to check on the girls. One of them hasn't checked in yet and I need to make sure she didn't get back into the drugs."

Sampson might be cold and brutal when it came to the business, but he had a soft spot for Pinky and the rest of the girls I had taken in. He had a daughter of his own that he was estranged from because of her own drug use. She ran off into the dead of night and he hadn't seen her since. He had a feeling she was dead somewhere, and there wasn't a damn thing he could do about it. It came as no surprise that he offered to come with me.

"I'm sure she just forgot to check in. If it's something serious then I'll give you a call," I promised, tiptoeing to give him a kiss on the cheek. I barely cleared his neck. "Love you."

"Love you, too," he said, giving me a gentle squeeze and pat on the butt.

I called Nia back once I was in the car. Her phone went straight to voicemail, but seconds later a text message came through telling me to come to Donovan's place. I gunned it, making sure I wasn't being followed, which was usually the case when I was out this late at night. There was no way in hell I would be able to explain what I was doing at Donovan's house this late at night, especially after an argument.

"Nia," I said to her voicemail, "Nia, please pick up and tell me you're okay."

She still hadn't replied when I pulled up to the apartment building. I grabbed Mercy from my glove compartment and placed her on my waist. The last thing I wanted was to get caught up in some shit fucking around with Donovan's bitch ass. I spent all this time pulling out my keys when the lobby door was broken. Not wanting to waste any more time, I entered the building in a mad dash, rushing up the stairs and creeping to the apartment door. I unlocked the door and let myself in, hitting the lights before I came in any deeper. Sobbing could be heard from deep in the house. I pulled Mercy out and kept her low as I crept deeper into the house. The crying grew louder the closer I grew to Nia's bedroom. I pushed the door open and saw her lying in bed, crying.

"Nia," I said, rushing to her side. I placed my gun on the nightstand and ran a hand through her hair to pull it away from her face. "Oh my—what the fuck!"

Essence poked her head up and laughed in my face. "Got you,

bitch!"

I went to grab my gun when a pair of strong arms wrapped around my neck, dragging me from the bedroom. I fought hard, dropping my weight and tugging away, but it was no use; this bitch had me tight and she wasn't letting go.

"Really," I wheezed to Nia. "After everything I've done for you?"

"Bitch, you thought I was gonna let you catch me slipping and get away with it? DONOVAN! She's here!"

Nia dragged me into my old bedroom where Donovan was waiting. He hopped off the bed and stalled off, punching me in the stomach and across the face. Nia cheered him on, even jumping up and down as this nigga beat the dog shit outta me.

"When I saw you in the salon, I told you that wouldn't be the last you saw of me, didn't I, you stupid bitch? You thought you could up and leave a nigga with no consequence and repercussions?" I moaned a reply, only to be met with a two-piece. "Wrong answer! Nia, let her go."

Nia shoved me to the floor as Donovan's foot lifted and kicked me right in the stomach. My vision was ebbing and fading, I couldn't breathe, and I could feel the rest of my body shutting down. I tried crawling away and thought I was successful, when I realized that Donovan was letting me run so he could drag me right back. He knelt over me, grabbed me by the hair, and slammed my face into the floor repeatedly.

"I thought I made myself clear that if I can't have you, then no one will. I made you, and you think you gon' walk the fuck away from me? I'll send you to hell with your old nigga before I let you walk these streets on another nigga's arm, embarrassing me!"

Donovan lifted my head to slam my face one more time, and I knew this was it: my nose was broken, which caused me to choke on my blood; my right eye had already swelled itself shut and my left was next; and nothing made sense anymore. I took the best breath I could and readied myself to meet my loved ones, when two shots popped off. Donovan's hold on my hair slackened, and I felt his weight disappear. My face hit the floor and stayed there, as I watched the scene in front of me. Nia ran deeper into the bedroom to hide, which proved futile as a masked figure crept into the bedroom, raised its gun, and popped two shots off. I couldn't see much, but I heard her crash onto the floor. I closed my eyes, praying that I wouldn't be next. They popped open as I was rolled over, and I knew I had to be dead or near death, because there was no way in hell my dead ex-boyfriend was hovering over me.

"Alonzo?" I choked out.

Lonzo bent down and pecked me on the lips. "I'll be back when the heat is gone. Stay safe, baby. Love you."

"Love you more," I said as his face grew faint, and my entire world faded to black…

TO BE CONTINUED…

ALSO BY TYA MARIE

CONNECT WITH TYA MARIE

Facebook: https://www.facebook.com/AuthoressTyaMarie

For exclusive sneak peeks join my **Readers Group: Tea with Tya Marie** https://www.facebook.com/groups/318594828537945/

Instagram: Tya_Marie1028

Twitter: LaTya_Marie

Looking for a publishing home?

Royalty Publishing House, Where the Royals reside, is accepting submissions for writers in the urban fiction genre. If you're interested, submit the first 3-4 chapters with your synopsis to submissions@royaltypublishinghouse.com.

Check out our website for more information: www.royaltypublishinghouse.com.

Text ROYALTY to 42828 to join our mailing list!

To submit a manuscript for our review, email us at
submissions@royaltypublishinghouse.com

Text RPHCHRISTIAN to 22828 for our
CHRISTIAN ROMANCE novels!

Text RPHROMANCE to 22828 for our
INTERRACIAL ROMANCE novels!